AM I A FOOL?

–

MARRIAGE EDITION

Also by Martin Eloke Chukwumah
In The Words Of My Father
Am I A Fool?
The Book Of Judas

Am I A Fool?
Marriage Edition

By

Martin Eloke Chukwumah

ISBN-13: 978-978-791-125-9

elokechukwumah@gmail.com
+234 (0) 9070364210

Table of Contents

PART 1

This Dishonourable Honourable

arriage is like an optical illusion. You see one thing before you enter, and after you do, you see a whole different thing that had been there all along but you never noticed it.

Marriage can be wonderful, it can also be painful. It is a coin of two sides, a world of two seasons, though in some cases, the dry season lasts the longest. I don't know how to describe my marriage. I really don't know. I am trying to be positive, to always see the good in any situation as my pastor would say. Joseph was sold into slavery by his brothers. But that was the beginning of his greatness. Jesus was betrayed by Judas, and that led to His sacrifice which has brought redemption to the world.

It is always darkest before the dawn, you would say. And I wonder if my dawn would come, or most importantly, if I will be alive to see it. You do not know me. I may be your next door neighbour. I may be your colleague in the office. I may be the wife of your very close friend. I may even be your relative.

For the sake of people involved, I will not tell you my real name. And all names have been changed to protect the identities of the people in it. But everything I say is true, I just haven't said it till now.

You can call me Kazima, I am forty three years of age, a mother of four, a daughter, a sister, an aunt, a business woman and a wife. You may observe that I called myself a wife last. That is because it pains me to call myself a wife. So let me take you back to when I was just a daughter.

I came back home one afternoon after lectures to find my father entertaining some guests. They seemed very chummy and I didn't want to intrude. The visit lasted longer than normal, so I went to eavesdrop.

"You must take me to the place you buy this drink from," my father's guest said. His name is Ahuk. He has an important role to play in this tale, but that will be later.

"Very well my good friend," said my father, whose name is Abaka. "When will you like me to take you there?"

"Ah Abaka, you know when."

"Ah, yes I do," said my father, then they both laughed.

They were former classmates and best of friends in their teens before Ahuk relocated to another state with his family. This was what I could glean before a touch on my shoulders startled me.

"Kazima, what are you doing?" asked my mother in a whisper. She is called Toru. I have never known her with a frown on her face. She is always a joy to be around and exquisitely beautiful. I guess any child would feel that way about their mother, but it is true, just ask my father.

"I am sorry Mummy," I whispered in return.

"Will you leave here immediately and stop eavesdropping," she censured, if it could be called that, because she had a smile on her face.

As I tiptoed away, I saw where our guests had hanged their coats and hats, then I knew what tribe they belonged to. It wasn't long afterwards when they left. Dinner time came, but my father had eaten, or drank to the brim. He was at the dining table though, looking at me from time to time smiling.

After dinner, he gave my mum a signal. She cleared the table which was my responsibility then left.

"Kazima," my father said. "Follow me to my study."

Oh goodness, what have I done this time? I asked myself as I followed him. I don't think my mother tattled, she never has. We, my brothers and sisters have that kind of relationship with her. If our father was given a brick for every secret our mother kept for us, he would have an estate by now.

"Kazima, please sit down," Abaka said, and I complied. "Do you know who came to visit me? That was Ahuk my best friend in my younger days and his son."

"Oh, really? That's nice," I said, with raised eyebrows like I was just getting the information for the first time.

"Do you know why they were here?"

"No father."

"They came because of a precious gem in my house."

"Gem? What gem?"

"You of course my silly girl. They came to ask for your hand in marriage."

There are places in the world where they have arranged marriages. But when you go there, they don't call it arranged marriage. They call it marriage.

"Me? But I am not ready to get married. Besides, you and I have had this conversation. I don't want an arranged marriage. I want to choose whom I will spend the rest of my life with."

"Kazima, listen very carefully to me." He clears his throat and sits upright. "The best kind of family is the one you don't choose. Think about it. I am your father right?"

"Right."

"I am not perfect. Your mother is not perfect. Your sisters and brothers, especially Kazime who annoys you is not perfect. But if you could choose, would you choose to be born into another family?"

"Absolutely not! I love you all, you are my family."

"I believe ninety percent of people would still choose their own family if they had a choice about it. But the other ten percent, for good reasons or not so good reasons, would choose a different family."

"But Dad, you know that such families begin with two people who have chosen themselves."

"Some times that is the true face, and some times that is a mask hiding what they truly feel inside because they still believe in soulmates, in destiny. Yes, they want free will to choose whomever they want. But deep down, they want it to be decided for them, to be arranged for them. And once they find their destined soulmate, they have a forever bound and can survive any storm.

I am not saying that arranged marriages are always the best. But when you compare, communities where marriages are by choice have a higher divorce rate than communities where marriages are arranged."

"That is true."

"Either way, it is not easy. Marriage is like a mirage; maybe that is where the name originated from, because it is not what you see from afar, but what you see when you arrive, and it may be better or worse than you imagine.

Marriage is something that mars you in age. Maybe that's how the name came about. Marriage is also…"

"I get the point." My father could go on and on making puns.

"I am just saying that you should consider it. His son is coming back next week Friday to take you out."

"Next week?"

"Yes. You will be ready wouldn't you?" said my father, which sounded more like it was a done deal than a question.

"Yes Daddy," I answered. Seeing that there was nothing more to discuss, I asked to take my leave. As I came to the door, I turned around and asked, "What is his name?"

"I think it is best for your future husband to tell you that himself."

Like lightning my fate was decided, and I had to wait till Friday to hear its thunder. My mother and my eldest sister Uroma were there with me as they helped me get ready.

"I don't know what is wrong with you children of nowadays," said Toru.

"Mum, I don't understand," said Uroma.

"You go on dates with strangers you meet on the internet. You don't know their background, their family and friends, even their names might be fake; all in the name of love and marriage. But when your parents say go out with this man or woman, or marry this man or woman from this good family we have known for years. You get angry and say we are archaic, backwards, old-fashioned. I will never understand you youths of today."

Uroma and I kept quiet, it is a fight we know we would never win.

"I remember the first time I met your father," our mother said. It is a story she has told and we have heard countless number of times. She always has a smile on her face every time she tells it. It is quite romantic. "My bride price had already been paid before I even set eyes on your father. He had just concluded his schooling and was on his way back to the country where a job was waiting for him. His father and my

father were business partners some time ago. And my fate was already decided before I was born.

Like you Kazima, I was nervous. I had never met the man I would spend the rest of my life with. He arrived safe into the country, but on his way home he had an accident. I had not seen him but I was deeply concerned. He came out with minor contusions so our wedding was not postponed."

I thank God for saving my father that day because He alone knows if I and the rest of my siblings would have been the children born of my parents.

"It is one of the happiest days of my life," my mother continued. "The first thing I noticed about your father when I first saw him was his eyes. He has kind eyes. I averted my gaze when I noticed that he had noticed me. Everything was done according to tradition and we went home as husband and wife.

We both respected each other and did what was expected of each of us. If you ask me when we fell in love, neither of us will be able to tell you. But what we will say for certain, is that we are one, he is me and I am him. We love each other with our whole being."

It is funny how my father tells the same story almost word for word when he gives his version of how he and my mother got married.

My date, or my prospective husband as my mother said, arrived thirty minutes early. This was a good sign, I thought; a man who is punctual. I didn't come out immediately to see him. That time was not for me, it was for him to try and bribe my mother. I mean that word in a good way. He bought for her gifts and presented items his mother bought for her, that was how prospective mothers-in-law bonded. The men bonded over other things, and by other things I mean food and drinks.

When my time came, I walked out. I looked calm, but inside me was a raging tsunami. This would be the first day of the rest of my life; the day I will tell our children and grandchildren about when I met their father and grandfather. He looked debonair in foreign attire while I was dressed in traditional attire. If I was looking for reasons to say we didn't match, here was it. He looked handsome and something about him reminded me of my father. He cleared his throat and spoke; the first words he spoke to me.

"Nice to meet you Kazima. My name is Dreka, Dreka Mubah."

There was a way he talked, he exuded confidence and class.

"Nice to meet you too Dreka," I said, as I imagined myself being called Mrs. Kazima Mubah.

"Shall we?" he asked, and I answered with a smile.

He took me to a nice restaurant. We talked and got to know more than just our names. I did find him fascinating and I bet the feeling was mutual because he didn't take his eyes off me the entire evening. He brought me back home thirty minutes before it would be ungodly. We made plans for our next date before he left. My mother and sisters couldn't wait to hear all that happened while my father just wanted to make sure that he treated me with respect and that I got home safe.

Dreka and I went out a couple of times more and I still wasn't certain that I wanted to marry him. But that changed on our sixth or seventh date when he introduced me to his friends as his fiancée. That was when I truly saw my future as Mrs. Kazima Mubah. I told my parents about my decision and they were elated. Things went fast after then. My father and Ahuk were like two kids again. Sometimes it was hard to tell who was happiest, we the betrothed or them the fathers-in-law.

I entered into my husband's house in my third year in the university a virgin, but I couldn't say the same about him. He worked as an aide to a senator which was a stepping stone to where he wanted to go.

"Someday," he told me. "I will become the president of this great nation."

I believe in his dream, not because I want to become First Lady, but because I want our children to be proud of their father, for him to leave a good legacy for them. I discovered I was pregnant a month shy of our first anniversary. I was just about to tell him when he told me that he had been invited to the house of a party member for dinner. He was so excited that I thought it best not to tell him then. It was impromptu which meant that we got there late because I couldn't find the right dress to wear.

Dreka was livid but he kept his suave nature. We were the last guest to arrive and my husband apologised repeatedly. You see, he had decided to run for city council, and our host and his guests were kingmakers so to speak.

A wife by the side of an aspirant or politician is actually a good campaign strategy which was evident at the dinner. The men talked politics, and we the women, well we talked politics, in our own way.

Dinner was served, everything looked delicious but I found them nauseating. It is funny how pregnancy affects women. I knew I was going to throw up, there was no stopping it. I just had to keep it in till I reached the toilet. But unfortunately, I puked over our host as I made my way to the toilet. I felt so embarrassed. If Dreka was angry before, now he had reached his boiling point. I apologised once, and just as I was about to apologise a second time, my tummy wambled and I knew it was coming. Luckily I made it to the bathroom then I vomited what I had for lunch.

The wife of our host came into the toilet to see how I was doing. It was obvious to her and the other women that I was pregnant. She told me not to worry about it and gave me her contact to call if I needed any assistance.

The journey back home was treated with silence on my husband's part. I apologised repeatedly but his face remained stern. He parked the car and then walked straight to the house. I still hadn't told him that I was pregnant, not in the mood he's in. I made my way into the house and I found him waiting for me by the door.

"Sweetheart I can explain," I said, then locked the door. And as I turned around to face him, that was the first time it happened. That was the first time he hit me.

"Do you know how much you embarrassed me out there?"

I was still in shock as I held my face. He slapped me a second time and then I fell to the ground.

"I will be a laughingstock among my colleagues. They will never give me their support now, all because of you. You, you silly…" he took his hand up to hit me a third time.

"I am pregnant!" I said, as I crossed my arms in defence.

"You are what?"

"I said I am pregnant, that is why I puked over your party leader."

"Oh, Kazima, I am so sorry," he said, as he knelt down beside me. "Please forgive me. I had no idea. You are pregnant? Wow! This calls for celebration."

Just a few seconds ago he was erupting like a volcano, but now he looked as happy as a child. I didn't know what to make of it. He lifted me from the ground into his arms and carried me round the sitting room in excitement. It seems he had forgotten what he just did, and for the sake of happiness, I focussed on the infant in my womb and not the elephant in the room.

He got the full support of the kingmakers. How could he not? When they learnt that his wife was expecting their first child. He called me a blessing, lady luck. My family and friends were so excited when they heard the news and I couldn't detract from it and tell them that he hit me.

As you might have guessed, he won the election in a landslide; the press dubbed him a rising star - the future of government. He was loved by his constituents and they showered me with the same love when I delivered my first child, a boy named Dreka after his father, whom his father said, would continue his legacy.

My husband Dreka Mubah was indeed a rising star, he was charismatic, and even without saying it, people know that he would one day become president. He made positive changes in our community, created more jobs, made laws that were actually beneficial to the people and not those in government for once. Contracts came and he executed them to completion. I was truly proud of him and had all but forgotten about that fateful day. But he gave me a reminder after he concluded his second term as councilman.

He was expecting to be his party's candidate for the forthcoming federal elections into the House of Representatives. But unfortunately, they chose another candidate. He was the top-choice and most loved by the people, but politics being politics, it was always a game. He was furious and I couldn't calm him. His mother Lakimi came in anticipation of the good news, but alas, we had to wait for the next election.

It was terrible at home. We had two children by now, the second is a girl. Whenever they were in school or out that was when Dreka showed his other side. There was a day I forgot to prepare my mother-in-law's food separate because she dislikes beans. I went to work and when I returned, I saw my husband pleading with his mother.

"What is the problem?" I asked, because I felt concerned, but my question provoked him.

"What is the problem? What is the problem?" Dreka said, as he walked up to me, and before I knew it, he slapped me three times and I fell to the ground. "How can you go to work without preparing something for my mother to eat? You know she doesn't eat beans."

That was when I realised my mistake.

"Sorry, I forgot. But that doesn't mean that you should hit me."

It seems every word out of my mouth provoked him. He hit me continuously and rained insults on me. I tried my best to shield myself, but it was pointless. I wanted to scream so that the children would wake up. Dreka is always on his best behaviour when his children are around. But I chose instead to bear the pain so they wouldn't see their father like this.

Feeling satisfied with his deed, he left me on the floor and went to our bedroom. My face was swollen. I had to hold my tears because it was more painful to cry. I picked myself up and sat on the closest chair. My mother-in-law was still there looking at me. Seeing that Dreka had gone, I felt free to speak.

"How can you sit there and watch your son beat his wife a fellow woman like you and the mother of your grandchildren?"

I had to speak my mind and didn't mind that catarrh was dripping from my nose into my mouth at that time. I was eager to hear her response, but she kept silent for what seemed like an eternity though it was two minutes.

"It serves you right," Lakimi said. "Next time, you do the needful before you go to work." She stood up and began to walk to her room. "Stop complaining that Dreka beats you. Is this the first time that a husband beats his wife?"

I couldn't believe my ears. What kind of family have I gotten married to? I slept in a guestroom but my husband came and bundled me back to our matrimonial bed, because married couples shouldn't sleep separately, as he said. The next day, Lakimi got her grandchildren ready for school. And after school, she went and picked them so that they could spend the rest of the week with their paternal grandparents.

No one wanted them to see me in my battered state, including me. But their absence meant that Dreka had all the time to beat me whenever he felt annoyed by my actions or inaction. A jobless man can be a very angry man. Two weeks later my children returned and not long after that, I discovered that I was pregnant, and this time, with twins. Their arrival brought serenity back to my home. But that was not all, we had double blessings. Dreka was appointed as a commissioner overseeing both the Youths and Labour ministries of the state. It was the aim of the government to integrate both ministries and they needed someone capable. Celebrations filled the streets, and people came to congratulate him, and Dreka never let the opportunity slide to tell them that his wife had given birth to twins.

Seeing that he has become a well-known public figure, Dreka instructed me to resign my job as a curator to protect our privacy. So I did. He asked me what kind of business I would like, one that I didn't need to leave home everyday.

"I would like to own an art gallery," I answered.

I had always wished to have one and I have garnered all the experience I needed from the national museum. He established two for me, so that people wouldn't be certain in which of the two they could find me. I found fulfilment in my work, all my children were artistically gifted in one way or the other, and this helped us bond more.

Dreka did such a remarkable job that he even became more popular than the governor. International organisations gave him awards. I was always with him at the award ceremonies. It didn't take long for the media to dub us the perfect couple in government, the example for everyone to emulate. It was our brand and opened doors for him and me also. I got foreign patrons in my galleries, soon my artists were exhibiting all over the world. I had to smile and make them believe that Dreka and I had the perfect marriage because behind the scenes, the abuse continued.

I never told my parents the abuse I suffered because like everyone, they were proud of and beguiled by Dreka. After five years working at the ministry which has now been merged into one, my husband got the ticket he had always wanted; the Federal House of Representatives. I was always by his side as he campaigned, we are the inseparable duo after all. The margin was close, but he won and we the family of Honourable Dreka Mubah moved to the capital.

We didn't know many people there, but we regularly entertained visitors, some with goodwill and others were professional brownnosers. Our families came to visit from time to time, and this made me feel safe because Dreka was on his best behaviour, as long as it was not his mother who visited. I opened another gallery and business was booming.

Dreka completed his first tenure with excellence. His re-election had little opposition, in fact, people wanted him to toss his hat in for the presidential race. But he told me that now was not the time. He had learnt from when he lost his first bid to the House of Representatives. His first and second tenures were used to grow his popularity and offers came from international organisations to be their head but he declined because of his dream; to become president.

"We are close Kazima, we are close," he said to me towards the end of his third tenure as an honourable representative.

I nodded and tried to smile as I nursed my cracked rib. Apparently I had no right to stop my children from spending their holiday with their paternal grandmother. I didn't go to work for two weeks, I didn't even leave the house. The doctor came and treated me. It was obvious to him the abuse I suffered even though my husband would say;

"My wife is quite clumsy."

When I felt better I resumed work but my mind and my heart wasn't there. This would no longer be my life. I had to take a stand, Dreka's disrespect of me, our marriage, must stop. If he ever hits me again I will hit back. My mind was made up. That night, I intentionally chose not to cook dinner because I wanted to have this fight with him. I wanted to stand my ground.

"What is this? What is the meaning of this?" said Dreka, as he stared into the empty plates on the dining table.

"We have to talk Dreka, we have to talk," I spoke with all the authority and strength I could muster. "I am not your punching bag. I am a human being. I am your wife, the mother of your four children. I am Kazima."

I could tell that he was surprised as I stood up to him. I have never spoken like this to him or anyone before in my life.

"I will no longer tolerate your abusive nature. Marriage is a union built on love and respect. But you have never loved or respected me."

Dreka began to laugh.

"I don't love you? If you know how much I love you, you would fall down on your knees and worship me," he said, in all seriousness. "No man has ever, or will ever love you like I do. You are lucky that you married me. If I was like some of my colleagues, I would have dozens of mistresses. But I have never, not even once, cheated on you, and for that you should be grateful."

"Is that all you promised me? Is that the sole vow you made on our wedding day?"

"I no longer want to hear this you ungrateful pig. I am going to our room, and you better come and join me soon."

He stood up and began to walk. One mind told me to let him go and continue the fight another day, but the other, just as Dreka walked passed me, told me that we must have this conversation tonight.

"You are not going anywhere," I said, as I pulled him.

The next thing I knew, he used his right leg and swept me off my feet, and before I reached the ground he slapped me twice with both hands. I was discombobulated, at least for a while, but then he reminded me where I was as he stomped and kicked me. Normally, he spoke in anger when he beats me. But tonight, he said nothing and let his kicks do the talking.

After a minute he stopped. He wasn't out of breath so I expected more. But instead of hitting me, he carried me on his arms into our bedroom and laid me on his side of the bed. He laid beside me, and without saying a word, he fell asleep. I was in pain and couldn't turn or stretch my body. If I could, maybe I would have ran away or I would have smothered him, but I didn't have the strength to do either. So in bed I lay next to my abuser.

Somehow I too fell asleep. I woke up the next day and most of the pain was gone. Dreka was not by my side. The aroma of something cooking found its way to our room. It smelled nice but I was more angry than hungry. I stood up from bed. I was resolute that Dreka and I must finish the conversation that was started last night. I walked out of the room, and as I made my way downstairs, I saw Dreka with a tray of food in his arms climbing the stairs.

"Good morning sweetheart," he said. "I prepared this for…"

I threw the tray out of his hands.

"What sort of disrespect is this?" he said, then he slapped me and threw me down the stairs.

I heard some cracks as I tumbled down. I landed on my belly and then I knew that something was terribly wrong. Dreka ran down the stairs like a thief who didn't want to get caught. He was a thief quite alright, and last night was when his ninety nine days ran out, and today was my day. He jumped down the last five steps and landed next to me. He continued from where he left off last night with a barrage of kicks. I was in so much pain and he was engulfed in rage that neither of us heard the door open.

I felt a gust of wind, but it wasn't because the door was opened, it was because my annoying brother Kazime ran to my rescue and kicked Dreka so hard that he flew a couple of feet away. Dreka wanted to get up but that was when he saw our parents and our children. They had wanted to surprise us but we were the ones who surprised them.

I couldn't speak. All I could do was stretch my hand to my brother for help.

"Dreka, what have you done?" Ahuk his father asked. I guess his wife never told him that this was a common occurrence in our household.

My children, all four of them were shocked, and I could see the disappointment Dreka felt for himself. My father wanted to take something and strike him, but he held himself back. My mother was in shock as my mother-in-law remained indifferent.

"We have to take her to the hospital," my father said. Then he turned to Dreka. "I regret the day I gave my daughter to you."

"You are a disgrace to your family," Dreka's father said. "How could you do such a thing to your wife?"

Dreka was now in tears as he knelt and pleaded. Kazime wanted to kick him one more time, but instead, he carried me in his arms and rushed to the car. It was when we got to the hospital that the doctor discovered that I was pregnant. Yes was, because I no longer am. The trauma to my stomach caused a miscarriage. I was heartbroken and so were the rest of my family and my father-in-law.

"Abaka, I am so sorry about this," Ahuk apologised. "I had no idea that this was what was happening in their marriage. It is my fault. I never should have brought my stupid son to ask for your daughter's hand in marriage."

"But she knew," I managed to say, as I pointed at my mother-in-law.

"Lakimi, you knew about this?" asked an enraged Ahuk. "You knew that our son was beating his wife and you didn't tell me to put an end to it?"

"How could you do such a thing?" asked my mother, and for the first time in my life, I saw my mother cry. "How could you sit back and watch a fellow woman be abused by her husband your son?"

"I am sorry, I didn't know what to do," Lakimi apologised, but she didn't tell them that she was an instigator.

"I am so disappointed in you Lakimi," her husband said. "I have never raised my hands on you, so how can you sit back and watch this atrocity happen?"

My thoughts exactly.

My father tried his best to remain calm. God only knows what he would do if he lost his calm. I stayed in the hospital for a week before I was discharged. My parents took me to the hotel room they stayed and where Kazime had been looking after my children. We were happy to see each other, they are my whole world. Dreka has been trying to reach us but my father has warned him to stay clear.

As I recovered in the hotel room, that was when we heard that Dreka had declared his intention of running for the seat of the president in the forthcoming elections.

"He may likely win," Kazime said. "The people love him, but they don't know that he is a monster. I didn't know myself. This would have been a happy day for us. I used to brag to my friends that my brother would become the next president. But now, I don't know what to say."

During the press conference, a reporter asked him this question.

"Honourable, where is your loving and supporting wife? Today is a big day for you and we are all wondering why she isn't here."

"Thank you," Dreka said. "Unfortunately my wife couldn't be here today. I never wanted to say this but, we suffered a miscarriage some weeks back and she is home resting."

"Oh, so sorry for your loss Honourable."

"Thank you," said Dreka.

Can you imagine? I agree, he didn't tell a lie to get points like most politicians. Instead he told the truth to garner sympathy for himself and get voters to support him. He used the pain he had inflicted on me as political gain. What kind of man did I marry?

Two days later there was a knock at the door. Kazime went and opened it and there he saw Dreka. He shot the door and locked it.

"I want to see my wife!" Dreka yelled. Someone had bought out the entire floor. Now we know who it was. "I want to see my wife!" he repeated.

My father was irate so he went to the door to put an end to this.

"You will never see her again," he said to Dreka.

"Fine, you can keep her away from me, but you can't keep my children away from their father. They are mine not yours." He paused for a while before he continued. "I am a powerful man, I could have soldiers come and take my children and put you in prison, if I so desired. But I came here alone."

My father closed the door but he left it unlocked. He came to me and for the first time in my life, I saw tears in his eyes.

"Please forgive me my daughter," he said. "If I had known that this is the kind of man he was I would never have asked you to marry him. Please forgive me, please forgive me."

"It is not your fault father, it is not. If I didn't marry him I wouldn't have had the children I have now."

"That is true. You have these children now, no one is forcing you to remain married to him. You can correct my mistake Kazima."

"Walk away from this marriage Kazima," my brother suggested. "He will not change. You were lucky. I saw the way he was beating you, you could have died."

"I need to see him. Let him in Daddy," I said.

They were both shocked, but I had to see him. Kazime was reluctant at first, but he obeyed our father and let Dreka in. They brought him to my room but didn't leave us alone. Kazime was gritting his teeth the whole time as he watched Dreka. Dreka knelt before me in supplication.

"Please forgive me Kazima, forgive me. Please come back to our home. Our bed, our home, my life is empty without you and our children." He turns and looks at my father and brother. "I promise," he said to them. "I promise you," he said to me. "I will never ever lay a finger on you again. Please forgive me. I have changed."

Kazime scuffed.

"Truly, I have changed. You don't know what kind of hell I am living in knowing that I might lose you. Please come back to me. Please come back home."

Maybe he was lying like the skilful politician that he is because he knows that with me by his side, he would appeal to a majority of voters. Or maybe he was being sincere and had no angle at all. I looked at my father, then my brother. I didn't need to say a word. My decision was clearly written on my face and their reaction too was glaring.

My children were out with my mother so they weren't here. But I had to think about them. Everything I do is for them. They are in their early and late teens. Dreka my firstborn has gotten admission into the university. And like his father had envisioned and groomed him, he wanted to go into politics like his father whom he so much looked up to. Once the news of our separation and divorce gets to the media and the reasons unearthed. It will cause a scandal that will live forever and tarnish my husband's reputation, his seat, candidacy and my son's future ambition.

Like I said, the names in this story were changed to protect the identities of those involved and prevent this scandal from getting out. I am one of many wives who suffer spousal abuse. This is my story, this is my life. I didn't choose my spouse, he was chosen for me. But that doesn't mean that arranged marriages are bad. All the marriages of my siblings were arranged. And none of them is abusive.

In the beginning I said marriage is like an optical illusion. You see one thing before you enter, and after you do, you see a whole different thing that had been there all along but you never noticed it. Now that you have discovered the truth, which may be good or bad, you can choose to walk away, accept it for what it is or view it like a Rorschach test - you see what you want to see. I have chosen to go back to my marriage, not because of my husband but because of my children. But still I wonder, AM I A FOOL?

PART 2

My in-law the Outlaw

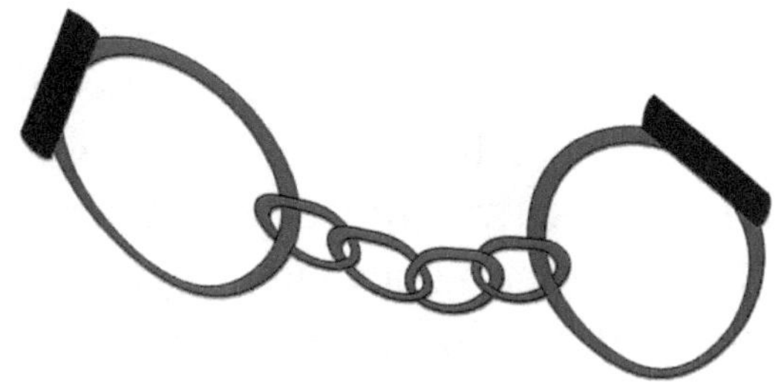

My in-laws, what have I done to you? I wish I had married an only child. How lucky are those who did, they won't have to deal with many in-laws like I do. I wish I was Chinese, they don't have much in-law problems. My people say, when you marry, you don't just marry a person, you marry their people and culture. My in-laws too have that saying but they add to theirs - In marriage, you don't lose a daughter, you gain a son. And that part they took very serious. If I knew then what I know now, my wife and I would have eloped as soon as we got married and never return.

My wife, oh how much I miss her. This year would have been our twenty fifth anniversary, but we lost her five years ago. Or maybe it still is. Because even though she is gone, I still feel married to her. My wedding ring still remains on my ring finger. She is everywhere I go. I see her smile in our son, and I hear her laughter in our daughter. My son is called Michael, he is fifteen; while my daughter is Deborah and thirteen years of age. Since the death of their mother I have tried to shield them from their maternal relatives, but those people know how to latch on to someone. They have even caused a rift between me and my family. Honestly, if I knew then what I know now, my wife and I would have eloped as soon as we got married and never return.

Before I continue my story I will like to introduce myself. My name is Samuel Gordon-West. I am sixty two years of age and a retired police officer living on my pension and what I make as a private investigator. I get consulted from time to time by the Service to help solve some cases. But recently they haven't brought any case to me, and I know why. It is because of my in-law, the outlaw.

My wife comes from a large family. Her father is called Alpha. He may be short but he carries the rage of six men and is easily irritated. And before I forget, he is seldom seen without a bottle in his hand since he was a baby. His first wife who is my wife's mother is called Alberta. She is the bane of my existence. Every breath that comes out of her is accompanied with an insult. My wife's stepmother is called Gemma, she only understands the language of money and is fluent in euros. She has six children of her own.

My wife had six siblings. The first is called Primus, and like his name, he is always the first, but from the bottom. After him is Secondus who is second to none when it comes to car theft. Next to him was Tertius who died at the age of thirteen in a gang war. He is followed by Quartus. I don't know much about him except that he travelled overseas a quarter of a century ago and calls at specific times of the day. The fifth is Quintus, he is the quintessential womaniser and has more children than he knows. He is followed by twins, Sextias my wife whom I called Sexy Sextias. She was the white sheep of the family and the only girl. Her twin is called Septimus, who is the criminal this story is about and a suspect to numerous crimes.

I was sitting in my office one afternoon watching a program when it was interrupted to a breaking story - The notorious Green Mask gang are in a shootout with the police as they tried to rob City Central Bank. They retreated into the bank where there are about twenty seven hostages as the reporter said.

"I think they will be finally caught this time," Paul, my partner said.

"I hope nothing happens to the hostages," Eliza my secretary said.

Somehow, one of the hostages was able to hid his phone and broadcast live what was happening. Six of the Green Mask robbers were spotted, but the seventh who was their leader hasn't been picked up by the camera. Everyone knew what the leader looked like. He too had a green mask but there was a black crow on it. He is the only lefty in the gang.

Soon the police commissioner came to negotiate with the robbers. He was my classmate in the academy and well respected. He walked to the front of the bank in a bulletproof vest and asked the robbers to make their demands. It was a distraction as a twelve man team were making their way through the back of the bank.

"We want you to take the barricade ten metres back. After you do that come and we will discuss more," said one of the robbers.

"Okay," said the commissioner, then he radioed his officers to do just that. "As a sign of good faith, I will ask that you release some of the hostages."

"Okay."

The door to the bank slowly opened. We watched in anticipation for the release of some hostages, but instead, the head of the gang came out with a shotgun and shot at the commissioner. Then everything went haywire. An explosion went off inside the bank and the hostages rushed out and it was difficult to tell them apart from the criminals. It rained bills on the streets and soon the barricade was breached as people rushed in to pick what they could.

In the midst of the mayhem the robbers made their escape in three separate cars.

"Oh no, they are getting away," complained Eliza.

"Don't worry, they will catch them," I said, but my thought was more on the commissioner.

The police took chase. News stations covered it with their helicopters. In the end, two vehicles were caught with five robbers in them while the third got away. It was during the evening bulletin while I sat in the living room with my children that the identities of the thieves were released. Their pictures were shown with their past criminal records. The two that got away were shown next. The first was a man known as Henry 'Butch' Sanders with a criminal record that could replace his full body tattoo. The second was revealed to be the leader of the gang and was no other than Septimus my in-law.

"I can't believe it. Dad look, its Uncle Septimus," Michael said.

I wasn't the least bit shocked, but I was angry to find out that he was the one who sent my friend to hospital.

"The police commissioner is in critical condition in St. Augustine's hospital as he suffered a brain trauma," the newscaster said. "We will update you as soon as we find out more on his condition. Meanwhile, the state has added the two escaped criminals to their Most Wanted list and have offered a reward to anyone with credible information that will lead to the arrest of these two."

Deborah my daughter began to cry. I wasn't sure if it was because of what he did or because he had been declared Most Wanted. She and my late wife had a soft spot for Septimus. In the days that followed there was no arrest and it was announced that the two robbers made away with five million.

In the second week of the manhunt, we got the news that Alpha my father-in-law had died and his funeral would be coming up in three days time. I left my children at home because I didn't want them around such reproachable people.

"You didn't bring my grandchildren to say farewell to their grandfather, you imp," said my mother-in-law. "If only you were man enough to get Sextias pregnant early, your children would be adults now and come to see their grandmother whenever they liked."

I have learnt that it is best to remain silent in such situations. Most of her grandchildren were there, but Michael and Deborah are the children of her only daughter.

It was a quick funeral with few attendees including the police officers that watched from afar. I went round and condoled every member of the family present.

"Sorry for your loss Primus," I said. "Sorry for your loss Secondus."

Gemma was the last person I met because she was surrounded by her son, her five daughters, their spouses and children.

"Sorry for your loss," I said to her, but she said nothing. I took out money from my pocket and placed it in her hand. "Please use this to pay some bills now that your husband is no more."

"Oh, thank you," she said, with a smile on her face.

I was just about to get back to my car and head back to work when Quintus held me by the hand.

"My stepmother wants to see you," he said, as he pointed at her.

I looked at my watch and hoped that whatever it was wouldn't cost me time.

"I will like you to drive me home," she said.

"Me? What about Primus? He lives close to you."

"I can't get in that rickety car of his. We will definitely arrive late but hopefully not late, if you know what I mean."

I looked around and saw that her children each had a ride home.

"What about your children? Can't one of them take you home?"

"Are you going to deny a widow your help?" She begins to cry.

I had no choice but to take her home and accompany her in for a tea of gratitude. The tea was quite hot but I drank it quickly so that I could get back on my way. On my fifth sip, I noticed a shadowy figure creeping at the back door.

"Shh," I whispered to Gemma, then I walked slowly to see who it was.

I grabbed a ladle which was the quickest thing I could find and hid behind the door as I noticed that the intruder was trying to force the door open. He picked the door open and walked in confidently. I was just about to tackle him to the ground then I noticed that it was Septimus. He saw me and was just about to speak when I twisted his right arm and tackled him face down to the ground.

"This is a citizen's arrest. Septimus I am taking you to the police station to answer for your crimes."

"I did not do it," he said, as he struggled in vain to get up.

"He didn't do it," Gemma said.

"What?" I asked.

"Rob the bank," she answered. "He was here with me the whole time."

"He was?" I said, as I lightened my weight on him.

"Yes I was," said Septimus, as he stood up. "That is why I asked her to bring you here."

"I don't understand. There is nothing I can do. Turn yourself over to the authorities and state your innocence."

"You and I know that they wouldn't believe an ex-con like me. I need undisputable evidence before I turn myself in."

"And that is where you come in," said Gemma.

"I don't understand."

"You are a private eye right?" asked Gemma. "Help him find evidence to clear his name then he will turn himself in."

"I still don't understand," I said.

Septimus and Gemma are not that close so I wondered why she was protecting him. Or maybe it is true, and he is indeed innocent.

"I am calling the police. You can corroborate his story."

"No no no, please Samuel, you have to believe me. I didn't do it."

I was just about to hit send when he said;

"Do this for Sextias. If she was alive she would believe me. In fact I wouldn't be in this mess because I would probably be with her during the entire heist and you wouldn't doubt my innocence."

He may be right, they spent a lot of time together. If Sextias was indeed alive, she would want me to hear him out. So I did. He confessed to being a former member of the gang and had taken part in some scores. But he vehemently denied being part of this recent heist. They were trying to punish him and let him take the fall for their leader Robert Hauser who was in the car with Butch.

"I will follow the threads you have spun and see what is on the other side," I said. I would get no help from my former colleagues because of my relationship with my in-laws. I and Paul would have to go about this as surreptitiously as possible. "I am doing this because of my wife," I said to both of them before I left.

I went back to the office and Paul and I got all the information on Robert Hauser.

"What is this about?" he asked me.

"I am afraid I can't tell you. If you are asked what you knew you could tell them that you know nothing."

"Plausible deniability."

"Exactly."

We went to Robert Hauser's apartment but he wasn't there. His neighbours said they haven't seen him for weeks, if they were telling the truth. We looked through the widow in search for any clue. It looked like a crack den. The only thing that was in good condition was the picture of him and his dog.

"We should check the dumpster," Paul suggested. So we did.

It is amazing what you could find out about people from what they throw away. Among what we found were cans of dog food, a takeaway pack from Isabel's something. The rest and the address were already smudged. We were leaving when I spotted a Saint Bernard come in through a not so obvious opening in the fence. It must be the dog in the picture, though it is much bigger now. It didn't bark at us but went straight to the trash and began scavenging.

"I think we should wait for the dog to be done then we can follow it to where it came from," I said.

Three hours went before the dog went back on its merry way. We followed closely behind and it led us to a building five blocks down. It went to the front of an apartment and began to bark. I heard the locks coming off.

"Hey, come in buddy," Robert said, as he opened the door and let the dog in. He looked around and when he saw us he closed the door quickly. Fortunately, we were able to push it open before he could lock it. He tried to run but Paul caught him. "I have nothing to give you," he said. "Take whatever you want from the apartment but don't hurt me."

"We don't want to hurt you," I said, as I motioned Paul to stand him up. "You are the leader of the Green Mask gang aren't you?"

"Me? Are you mad? Septimus is the one you are looking for not me."

"You have something to hide," said Paul. "If you didn't you wouldn't have run away when you saw us."

"Who sent you? Did he send you to kill me? What are your names? I want to see your badges."

"Our badges? Why do you…"

He knocked Paul down and ran out of the apartment. He was very fast even for Paul. He went through the alley and disappeared.

"We have lost him," Paul said to me when I caught up with him.

"We should go back to the apartment, there will be clues there," I said, and just then we heard gunshots.

We followed the noise and the crowd and then we saw the lifeless body of Robert on the floor riddled with bullets. Two officers were standing next to his body.

"What have you gotten me involved in?" Paul asked me.

"Plausible deniability, remember?"

We chose not to go back to the apartment lest suspicion fall on us. We went back to the office to find it locked with a note from Eliza on the door informing us that her child was in the hospital. We chose to retire for the day. On my way home I kept on thinking what had happened, and the fact that I have gotten nowhere with my investigation.

"Welcome home Daddy," Deborah said to me.

"Thank you dear. Where is Michael?"

"He left home around one and he isn't back yet."

I looked at my watch, it was half passed five. Michael didn't return home until seven.

"Where have you been?" I asked, as soon as he returned.

"You wouldn't let us go to the funeral so I went to see them afterwards," Michael replied in a curt manner. He walked up to his room before I could say anything. He has become very broody of late, teenagers.

The next morning he was out before I could make breakfast.

"He went to see Tommy. I think they are working on their mixtape or something," my daughter said.

He came back home three hours later looking gloomy and went straight to his room. I asked my neighbour to look after them then I went back to the office. Neither Eliza nor Paul were there when I arrived, so I fixed myself a cup of coffee and continued with my investigation. There was a faint unfamiliar smell in the office that day. Not bad, just different. I opened the windows and this helped me think clearer. I decided to go to the scene of the crime alone. I didn't want to involve Paul any further.

City Central Bank has gone back to business as usual. I walked in under the pretext of opening an account. After making my inquiries and observations, I left. I decided to take a walk and follow the thieves' escape route. The scene where the first vehicle was caught wasn't far from the bank. There wasn't much I detected there so I went to the next which was farther away but unfortunately there was nothing I deduced there too. Clueless, I decided to head back but then I saw a little girl who looked like my wife crossing the road with her mother. I followed them with my eyes and watched as they entered a restaurant called Isabel's Delight. Then I remembered that I had seen that symbol in the dumpster in Robert's house. So I crossed the road and went in. I took a seat then a waiter came over.

"What would you like for today?" she asked me.

I looked at the menu they had and said;

"Give me your special for the day."

"Anything else?"

"No, that would be all for now. Thank you."

The restaurant was far from the bank but there has to be a connection. So I waited. And while I waited, I learnt that the police commissioner had recovered and was stable.

I ordered my third meal of the day and was just about to leave after eating when the reward for my patience walked in. It was one of the cashiers in the bank.

"Do you have my package?" she asked a worker behind the counter.

"Of course Amber. I have your favourite right here," he said, as he hands her a takeaway pack.

"Thank you," she said, as she paid. "You are a lifesaver. Today was hectic."

She leaves and I follow behind. I kept my distance so as not to be noticed. She stopped at a bus stop and soon afterwards the bus arrived. I boarded after her still remaining inconspicuous and we bussed to her area and alighted. It was the same area Robert lived. I was the least bit shocked when I discovered that she lived in the apartment where we found Robert.

I waited outside the apartment for ten minutes and watched her shadow move from room to room. I wanted her to be relaxed before I question her. So when I saw that she was, I went and knocked at the door.

"Who is it?" she asked.

"My name is Samuel Gordon-West. I am a private investigator. I will like to ask you about the robbery that took place in your bank."

A moment of silence followed afterwards then she said;

"I have told the police everything. What more do you want from me?"

"I just need you to answer a few questions and after that I will be gone." I paused then continued. "I think it is best we have this conversation inside."

Another moment of silence followed before I heard her unlocking the door.

"Thank you," I said, as I walked in.

The dog was there and it seemed to remember me.

"How can I help you?" she asked.

"I know that you are an accomplice to the robbery," I went straight to the point. "I know that Robert was hiding here with you."

Her eyes and mouth were open as she probably wondered if she should confess or deny everything.

"I am just shocked that the police haven't linked him to this apartment because he died just a few blocks down."

"What do you want? You want money? I can give it to you. They threatened me. I had no choice," she said, but it was obvious to both of us that she was not as convincing as she hoped. "Who sent you? Is it the commissioner? Does he want Robert's cut?"

I wanted to ask more questions, but I realised that it was best to keep quiet and let her answer the questions I didn't know to ask.

"I had no idea that they were going to shoot him. Did he send you here to kill me? Please don't kill me. I told the police nothing, I swear. Besides, they work for him. Does he want his cut? Because I can get it for you. Robert hid it inside the chair. I can rip it up and get it for you." She begins to throw the throw pillows away. "Please don't kill me. I was going to take it to Club Hex I swear."

"Stop," I said. "You should… you should… take the money back to the bank and say you discovered it hidden somewhere."

"But what about the commissioner?"

"Don't worry, I will handle that."

I turn to leave then she asked;

"Who did you say you are again?"

I stopped and looked at her but I said nothing. When I was a few blocks away and certain that no one was following me, I called home. There was no answer so I called my neighbour. She answered and I told her that I would be coming home late. Deborah was with her, but Michael was not. He was working on his demo as he told her.

Club Hex was far and luckily it was on the route where I parked my car. So I drove the rest of the way. I parked at a distance and watched as I planned my next move. Then I saw the two officers who shot Robert arrive in their car. They gave their key to the valet and walked in. I removed my jacket to look as casual and inconspicuous as possible. Then I drove up, gave my keys to the valet and walked in.

The officers went to the VIP lounge so I couldn't follow them. Fifteen minutes later they came out with two well-dressed fellows and exited the club. I waited for their cars to be returned to them before I came out. Luckily the valet brought my car quickly and I was able to catch up with them.

A time came when we arrived on a desolate road. I turned off my headlights so as not to be spotted by them. They came to some abandoned warehouses and then drove into one of them. I parked and followed on foot. I heard the voice of a man as soon as I walked in. It sounded familiar and as I walked closer than I recognised who it was. It was Secondus.

"Normally I wouldn't be here today," he said. "But I made an exception because of my new pledge. He is my progeny and I know you all can testify how good he is."

This was an initiation. Five hooded initiates were in the middle with Secondus in front and surrounded by twenty other men or so.

"He is joined by four equally talented boys," Secondus continued. "They all completed the tests assigned to them and so have become worthy to become members of the Blood and Axe gang. Step forward and reveal yourselves."

The five pledges did as asked. The first person I saw was Tommy which shocked me. But my whole world crumbled when I saw the person next to him. It was my son Michael. I wished I could scream and tell him not to do this, but that would only cause more problems. I decided to leave, the sight of everything was heart-breaking. I have failed as a parent, I have failed his mother.

I went back home and waited all night for Michael to return, but he never did. The next morning I asked Deborah to go over to our neighbour's. Michael returned a few minutes after ten.

"Where have you been?" I asked.

"Didn't she tell you? I told Natalie that I was in the studio," he lied, confidently.

"Come here."

He wasn't his gloomy self. There was confidence in his steps.

"I know where you were Michael," I said, and he looked at me like I couldn't possibly. "I know that last night you were initiated into the Blood and Axe gang."

This caught him by surprise, just like Amber.

"I was there, I saw the whole thing. Why would you do this? Why would you bring disgrace to the memory of your mother?"

He began to tear up.

"I know I have not been around much since we lost your mother. But we are your family, not them."

His tears flowed freely now.

"How did you come about them? It was your uncle Secondus wasn't it?"

"Yes, and Uncle Septimus too."

"You see why I didn't want you or Deborah to associate with them. We have to get you out of that gang."

"It is not that easy, especially after I had completed the tasks they assigned to me."

"What tasks?"

"They asked me to make a duplicate of your office keys, copies of your certificates when you were in the academy, your bank details and other stuffs you carry on your person. They say if I am able to accomplish this, then they would know that I am worthy to become one of them."

"And you gave all these to Secondus."

"Yes, him and Uncle Septimus."

"I need to go to the office immediately. Go and meet your sister next door and no matter what, don't come back home until I do."

"Dad is anything the problem?"

"Don't worry about it. I will handle everything," I said. How can I tell him what I suspected?

I drove to the office as fast as I could. I opened the door and began to search. There must be a reason why they needed my office keys.

"Sir is everything alright?" Eliza asked.

"I don't know yet. But don't touch anything."

Fifteen minutes later Paul arrived and I gave him the same instructions. I didn't discover anything missing. Maybe they made copies or left something behind. So I continued my search. I started from the bottom then I made my way to the top as I searched the ventilation ducts and that was where I found it, a bloodstained bag filled with cash, guns and cartridges.

"How did this get here?" asked Paul.

"My thoughts exactly," said Eliza.

I didn't want to explain to them so as not to implicate my son. The bag was still in my hands when the police came in with a search warrant.

"We are here to…" one of the officers who shot Robert was saying as he saw me. "It seems you have done our job for us. Officers, take him into custody. Mr. Samuel Gordon-West, you are under arrest for masterminding the crimes committed by the Green Mask gang. You have the right to remain silent…"

I didn't know what to think as he read me my Miranda rights. Eliza was confused, so was Paul. The true criminals cuffed me and led me away. I didn't ask for or call my lawyer. How could I when they had all the false evidence they needed.

"We found your prints and documents in the home of Robert Hauser," said my arresting officer.

"You have eluded the authorities for years. I know about your time in the service. You were well respected, but if they only knew who you truly are."

After five hours of interrogation I gave up my right to remain silent.

"I need my phone call."

I called Paul and asked him to take care of my children and not to give them much detail, and to call my lawyer. I needed to pass information to him so that he could solve this case and clear my name.

The next day my lawyer came and I gave him the necessary information to give to Paul. During our meeting he told me that Septimus had been cleared as a suspect, and that Robert Hauser was named the leader of the group. Butch was still in the wind and the search for him had intensified.

"It will be difficult to clear your name. They have you dead to rights. I will tell Paul to locate Amber from the bank. Her testimony might set you free though it will implicate her as an accomplice which makes me doubt how cooperative she will be. But she is our best bet."

"Thank you, please do your best."

I was taken back to jail and there I remained for five days until men from the Federal Crimes Division came to my cell and said;

"Come with us Mr. Gordon-West."

My belongings were returned to me and I was driven to their office to meet the head of internal affairs, Lars Mulligan. Three agents were with me in meeting room C when he arrived.

"Tell me about your in-law Septimus," he went straight to business.

"He is the mastermind of this whole thing. I am innocent, truly."

"We know you are, otherwise we wouldn't have arranged your release. We need to know all about Septimus. We caught his stepmother who is also his accomplice as she tried to flee the state. She is not forthright with information on his whereabouts as he is now a fugitive."

I had a suspicion, though tiny, that Gemma was involved somehow. And it turns out that I was right.

"Please, explain to me what is going on. I have been in a cell for days."

"Officer Gerald, please come in," said Lars Mulligan.

In walked Henry 'Butch' Sanders with a bandaged head and a sling.

"This is special agent Gerald Hunt of our undercover unit. He was deep undercover investigating the corrupt practices of our police officers."

"Nice to meet you," said Gerald.

"Same here," I said. "I had no idea. But you were declared Most Wanted."

"That was because I was shot by Septimus who believed I was dead. Let me explain to you what happened. (He sits down) There was a power tussle in the gang. The commissioner wanted Septimus out and replaced with Robert Hauser. But Septimus wouldn't have it. He stole Robert's plan and organised a heist in City Central Bank against the commissioner's approval. Things escalated quickly and Septimus shot him so as to take power."

"Septimus was at the bank? But the shooter was a lefty."

"Not really. Septimus is ambidextrous."

"Oh yes! That's true. I completely forgot."

"I almost broke cover then to arrest him but I continued because I didn't have all the necessary information. All that I knew then was what Septimus told him; that the mastermind was a police officer who graduated from the academy the same year you did. It was while we escaped that he told me he just shot the head of the operations. And that he would have to share what we stole with Robert as recompense for stealing his plan and to buy his loyalty. I waited until we were safe and sound to make the call to my handler. Septimus had gone out so I brought out my phone from where I was hiding it to call my handler with the information. When I got through, the first thing I said was that I knew the head of the operation, and that was when Septimus walked in."

"Your cover was blown," I said.

"Yes and I couldn't deny it. He shot and grazed me in the arm. He shot again but missed. I couldn't fight back because I was bleeding in the arm. I took a bag of money and threw it at him then I ran out of the building. He chased after me. We chose a deserted place as our hideout so no one saw or heard anything. I saw another empty building so I hid there. I guessed I left a trail of blood and he found me. I had nowhere to run but to the top of the building to evade his shots. I was just about to make it to the tube to take me down when he shot me at the back and I fell down from the building. And that's all I remember."

"Luckily," said Lars Mulligan. "His handler knew their hideout and came just in time to save him. Septimus must have left believing that he died. He was in a coma for weeks and when he woke up he told us everything and we knew that Septimus had framed you."

"He knew that you hadn't revealed the identity of the ring leader," I said. "And that all you knew before that day was that he graduated from the academy at a particular time and was an officer who could have retired."

"Yes," said Gerald. "There are eleven of you from your set still in this city. You fit the profile, so he framed you. He figured that there will be an investigation, so he made nice with the boss and together with the corrupt officers they framed Robert as the head of the gang and you as the mastermind to take the fall."

"Thank the heavens that you woke up," I said, with a smile on my face.

"Yes, thank God. We have apprehended all the culprits except for Septimus who is in the wind. We will get him, it is just a matter of time."

"Yes you will, and I will help in any way I can."

"You are free to go Mr. Samuel," said Lars Mulligan. "We will contact you if we need anything else."

"Thank you," I said to both of them then I shook their hands.

An agent accompanied me out of the building. I am very happy to be free and cleared. My in-laws, what have I done to deserve this? I hate my in-laws but I love my wife. I love her so dearly and did what I did because of her. But now I wonder, AM I A FOOL?

PART 3

The Headmistress
my head mistress

My father's wife and my mother's husband are having an affair. I caught them red-handed in her office as they were… sorry I can't say it because the sight of them together is very irritating.

"Adanma," my step-mother mumbled. Her mouth was still ajar but she could not say any words.

Instead of waiting to hear whatever disgusting thing she wanted to say to me, I quickly ran out of the office as I heard her stumble to her feet. I wanted to go back to my class but I knew that she would find me there. Where do I hide? I wondered. It must be somewhere quiet where I can… Yes, I will hide in one of the bathroom stalls. I turned my back to make sure that she wasn't behind me which thankfully she wasn't. So I made a beeline to the girls' bathroom. You would always find at least one person there but luckily for me, it was empty.

I got into the last stall and climbed on the toilet seat so that no one could see my feet. I closed my eyes as I wished that I hadn't seen what I saw, but instead the picture became clearer in my mind. I yelled, but then I covered my mouth. This was my hiding place and I couldn't risk being discovered because I don't want to face the reality out there. How do I tell my father? How do I tell my mother? Their spouses are cheating on them with each other.

My name is Adanma as you know, my full name is Adanma Regina Ezeugo, the first and only daughter of Architect Vitalis Ezeugo and Doctor Regina Adedotun. Yes, my mother and I share the same name. I am the apple of her eyes as she calls me, and the sugar in my father's tea, as he calls me. Sadly, I only have two elder brothers, Nnabuike and Tolu. They are both in university.

I am sixteen years old, and the most valuable piece in the chess game our divorced parents play, or the rope in their tug-of-war if I am being literal here. I remember the day they separated, I was ten then and didn't realise what was going on. My brothers had taken a side; they chose to be with our father. I on the other hand just watched as they argued and as our mother packed her things and mine.

"You are not taking my only daughter," my father said to my mother. I remember those words clearly.

"I am not leaving without her," she said, as she picked me up.

I wanted so bad to stay with my father, as you well know; girls love their daddies. I stretched my hands towards him and he grabbed me.

"You have the boys," my mother said, as she pulled me to her side. "I am not leaving without my daughter. I am not leaving without Regina."

If my father wanted, he would have pulled me to his side. But instead, he chose to let me go. And till this day, I bear feelings of resentment towards him. Don't get me wrong, I love my mother and she takes good care of me. I just felt that he should have put up a stronger fight to keep the only sugar in his tea.

"Hello, is anybody here?"

That is unmistakeably the voice of my class rep, Violet. Not only is she my class rep, she is also my best friend. I remain silent, I wasn't ready to come out yet.

"Reg, are you here?" Reg, that's what she calls me. It seems everyone have their own nickname for me. "If you are here please come out. I am missing biology class because of you."

She wants to become a doctor like my mother who has been mentoring her. I don't like the fact that she is missing her favourite subject but I know that if I come out she will ask what is wrong with me, and that, I can't say, not even to her. How I wish I never saw what I saw. I am in a dilemma between Lucifer and the Grim Reaper. If I keep it in, I will implode. If I tell my parents, I will crush their hearts.

The bell for recess rang which tells me that I would soon be discovered. It is better I blend into the crowd. So I leave the toilet. I faced down as I walked the hallways. Where I was going, I don't know. I couldn't go home with my stepfather. Now I know why he likes to pick me up. Maybe I should make a run for it to my father's house. But then he would ask why I came when it wasn't his day with me.

The life of a child from a divorced home is very difficult and complicated. The divorce rate in Nigeria is very low. Studies say that 0.2% of men and 0.3% of women are divorced. I am the only person in school whose parents are divorced. No one can relate to the pains I go through. And it seems, that I am about to go through another divorce, double the dose this time.

I look up and realise that I am back at the toilet. In my confused state I must have gone round in a circle.

"Regina Ezeugo," my biology teacher calls. "Where have you been? The headmistress is looking for you. Come with me."

I couldn't escape and I couldn't explain why I hid myself. So I just followed him. We came close to the parking lot on our way to the headmistress' office. I was relieved to see that my adulterous stepfather's vehicle wasn't there.

"Wait here," my teacher says to me, as he went to meet the secretary.

They spoke for a little while then she allowed him into the office of my equally adulterous stepmother. My heart pounded as I thought what could happen when I am asked in. I honestly don't know what to say, and I don't know what she could possibly say to me.

"You can go back to your class," my teacher says to me, which brought me back to reality.

I didn't waste any second there. I went back to class and for the rest of the day, I said no word to anyone, not even when I was asked questions in class. The closing bell rang, and I wasn't sure which of my step-parents I would be going home with. I watched as parents came and picked up their wards until I was the last person there. It seemed intentional as I saw my stepfather drive in. He probably didn't want to cause a scene. He parked his car a few feet away from me. I stare at him in anger and he stared back. I truly wish I could step up and step on my stepfather.

I am having an affair with the wife of my wife's ex-husband. Well, I don't know if you can call it that since she is one of many. But of all my mistresses, the headmistress is my head mistress. You can call me Mr. Williams. I never get to first-name basis with any of my mistresses or people like you I don't trust as I am sure that you want to expose my illicit ways.

I am a highly libidinous erotomaniac and I have to feed the beast regularly, if you know what I mean. I am very clandestine with my affairs. I play it smart and always use protection. Most men don't know how to play this game. In order to avoid suspicion, shower your wife with love, love her and continue loving her. That is the magic chword - LOVE. It works for wives and mistresses.

A time came in my life when I realised that I needed to get married. None of my paramours at the time did I want to 'settle down' with. They all wanted children, and I really don't. So I found a divorcee with three kids which was perfect for me. At first she turned down my advances, saying that she just got out of a nasty divorce and wasn't in the right frame of mind to date anyone. But I persisted, and of course, I showered her with love.

"You are very romantic," she would say to me. "The romance had died in my former marriage."

We courted for three years before she agreed to marry me. I had exactly what I wanted; a wife who is all mine and three stepchildren who I was hardly responsible for.

I was faithful to her in our first year of marriage so as to cement the trust she has in me. It wasn't easy taming the beast. My wife doesn't do things I like in the bedroom. Yes, missionary is fine but it doesn't give me any head way to where I want to go. Finally I decided to unleash the beast. Well, let's just say that the ladies didn't find it easy. My phone was constantly ringing because they all wanted an encore. I never ask for their native names. I always ask for their English names. So Ruth's name on my phone is saved as Rutherford. Nancy is saved as Nelson, Juliet is saved as Julian and so on. It was an unspoken rule between my wife and I; we never go through each others phones.

The headmistress' phone number is saved in my phone as Head mistress. I mean, the name is there but my wife never suspected it anytime she sees her call. I remember the first time I met her, oh, what a tamed beauty. She was already married to Vitalis at that time, but I couldn't take my eyes off her. Adanma was having a birthday party and that was when Regina decided to test and see if I and her kids would have a good relationship.

I was introduced as her work friend and I played my role to perfection. Vitalis on the other hand knew exactly who I was and scrutinised me with his judgemental eyes. It was the headmistress who kept me company for most of the party.

"It is difficult trying to find your place or assert yourself into a divorced family isn't it?" she asked me.

"Yes it is. No matter what you do the kids will never trust or respect you."

I found her very alluring, especially when she told me that she was a headmistress. I know that I am not the only guy who has fantasised about sleeping with their teacher or headmistress. Here was my opportunity, and that was when I decided that she must be mine.

When Adanma was admitted into her school, I saw this as my opportunity. I insisted on picking her up most of the time.

"I want to develop a good relationship with Adanma," I would tell my wife.

"Oh, that's lovely," she would say, and indeed it was.

The headmistress and I would make dinner plans to talk about the difficulties of being a stepparent. That was when I decided to seduce her. I showered her with attention and she called me whenever she was having problems with the children.

On the day I lived my fantasy, she called, sad, saying that one of the boys was rude to her. I asked that we meet at the hotel where we usually talk about our problems and she came. She had no choice, she had to succumb to my wiles, and that was when I realised that she had a tamed wild side.

Weeks went by without her speaking a word to me. But then she called me and well, you know the rest. We did it anywhere and everywhere. My favourite spot was in her office which was my ultimate fantasy. She is the most adventurous and experimental of all my mistresses. I mean, she was new to the game but she taught me things I never knew and took me to heights of pleasure I never knew existed. Her husband is indeed a big fool.

Unfortunately we took a hiatus when I got married. We saw each other constantly. She wanted me but I ignored her, and in case you don't know, ignorance is the best aphrodisiac for women. When I decided to go back to my real self, she was my first call, and we caught up on lost time. My other mistresses were not left out. The beast was well fed.

Sometimes I forget how many mistresses I have. Some of them are actually married. They are the best kind because they keep everything secret. The rest are single. I carefully choose those I tell that I am married. They don't really care since they have other men and as long as I do my part of taking care of them financially. Then the remaining, I call them the hopelessly romantic fools who honestly believe that I want to marry them.

In all my dealings with the opposite sex, I have discovered that there are two types of women. The first are women who value truth. To them, nothing is as romantic as honesty, and nothing is as heart-breaking as lies. And that is the kind of woman my wife is. But there is a subcategory under this, and these are women who can accept you for who you are - vices and all. You may lie to the whole world, sleep around, but they want to be that one person whom you always tell the truth.

The second type of women are the artificial and vain ones. Hardly anything about them is real. They value lies, nothing is as romantic as the false life you live and the lies you confidently tell them. You can never win them with the truth. Lie and lie and lie, that is the only way to get them. These kind of women mostly become mistresses and trophy wives.

I choose women from these categories carefully, and I have been able to keep my secret secret. But now, as I look out my windscreen at my stepdaughter, I really don't know what to do. If she tells my wife, my life is ended. I don't want to leave the perfect life I have. I honk my horn, but she refused to come or move. I honk for a second time and still there was no movement.

"I have to go to her," I say to myself. But be subtle, my inner voice said.

I come out, and walk slowly towards her. Luckily she didn't move or run away. What do I say to her? I kept wondering until I was next to her. Still no words came out of my mouth. We stood there in awkward silence then she walked to the car, and I followed behind. After we had settled in and fastened our seatbelts. I turned to her and said, or pleaded would be the right word.

"Please don't tell your mother. It would be the death of her."

She looked at me for a brief second and it looked like she agreed with me.

"Please don't tell your father either," I said, and observed a slight nod as her eyes became teary.

I was relieved and I promised myself to never do it again; that is get caught.

I am having an affair with the husband of my husband's ex-wife. I know what you think, you think I am evil. Maybe I am. I never intended it to go this far. I never intended for us to get caught either. I am filled with shame and regret. I hope Adanma doesn't tell her father, this will definitely end my marriage. No one in my family on both my parents' sides has gotten divorced. I am the last to get married among my siblings and for it to end because of infidelity on my part barely five years in would definitely kill my mother.

I wish I could turn back the hands of time. There weren't many suitors, or men who were genuine. Maybe they were intimidated by my education. I knew of the family of Arc. Vitalis Ezeugo. His sons were in my school and I knew when their parents got divorced. Vitalis and I spoke from time to time concerning his children until it became a little personal. In him I saw a lonely soul like myself. He couldn't believe that his marriage had disintegrated.

"No one cheated," he told me. "We drifted apart, at least that's what my wife, I mean ex-wife Regina says. We had been arguing a lot. She said that she had lost herself in our marriage and wanted to discover who she was once again. I no longer made her happy or fulfilled. I tried to make it work because I didn't want to lose my family but then, tragedy stroke."

I knew of the tragedy in his family. I and some members of staff paid his family a condolence visit.

"My son, our first son died in a bus accident. And from then, things deteriorated and there was no salvaging our marriage. She loves all our kids, but she had this special connection with her firstborn son. And after his death, she couldn't bare looking at me in the face because I remind her of him. She could no longer stay in the house because it reminded her of him.

I had to let her go. I had to let her grieve in her own way, even if it meant that my family would break."

I truly felt sorry for him. We became closer from that day. I usually don't get that close to the parents of my students, but I liked him, and I could tell that he liked me too. We began dating and it didn't take long for him to ask for my hand in marriage. I was surprised but then I realised that he always saw himself as a husband and a father, he didn't know how to live otherwise.

It was a grand wedding, my mother made sure of that. It was the happiest day of my life. His ex was invited of course, but she didn't attend of course, which reinvigorated her children's disapproval of course. But that wouldn't spoil my day because I would soon have children of my own.

We were keen on getting pregnant as soon as possible but five years have gone by and we haven't been able to conceive. We have tried many things and coitus has become a chore, a boring routine of the same position to maximise the chances of conception. The doctor said nothing is wrong with either of us, but all eyes were on me since he has three children to prove his virility.

I want to have children of my own. To be called Mrs. Somebody is not all I want. I want to be known as Mama Somebody. It is an unofficial title where I come from. Honestly, most people don't know my name. It is funny how some people forget to ask my name or don't remember it. I take care of everybody's children and they don't remember or ask my name. Even in church I am known as the Headmistress. I walk and work unnoticed and invisible. Mr. Williams is the first to truly notice me. In him I found a friend and companion. Like me, he was hated by our stepchildren. And like me, he and his wife have been trying to have a child, or so he made me believe.

I honestly didn't intend it to go this far. I was in a vulnerable state and he took advantage, or maybe I gave him the advantage. I didn't pull back or resist; I just wanted to be comforted. I went back home. I didn't know what to feel, I had opened a door I never thought I would, or I had eaten the forbidden fruit. But in the days that followed, I found myself fantasising about Mr. Williams. I wanted his touch, I wanted to surrender myself to him.

It might have been a mistake the first time, but now I indulged myself. There is a way he talks to me that I find very alluring. He is a vigorous and creative lover. He does things to me that my husband wouldn't try or imagine. Yes, missionary is fine but I can't linger when I want more gusto. It was like I had been starving myself all these years, and now that I had the opportunity, I inundated myself. I came up with the most crazy ways and places, even Mr. Williams was shocked. I wish I could be like this with my husband. I no longer cared about having children, I just wanted to pleasure myself. But if I had controlled myself, maybe, I wouldn't be in this situation.

My husband greeted me when he returned from work, which told me that Adanma hadn't exposed our affair. I kept my phone close because Mr. Williams said he would take care of it. It was late in the night when I got his message. It was a text that said; IT IS HANDLED. I deleted it immediately.

Adanma refused to spend the court-assigned days with her father. He was worried and asked me to talk to her in school, which I couldn't but told him I did. I avoided her like a plague. Mr. Williams never came to pick her up after school. If I could, I would avoid them for the rest of my life; if only I could.

The anniversary of the death of my husband's first son was coming up. And it is their tradition, and now mine because I am married to him, to go to church and give thanksgiving and visit his gravesite. His other sons, Nnabuike and Tolu came back from the university, they never miss it.

I thought about feigning illness but I didn't want to disappoint my husband anymore or give my stepchildren more reasons to hate me. It is just one day, I thought to myself, then the unfortunate happened. The first case of COVID 19 was reported in our state. The next day, over a hundred cases were discovered. The government declared a complete lockdown for fourteen days to contain the spread of the virus. I thought I had escaped the dreaded meeting with Adanma, but I was wrong.

"I am thinking of something," Vitalis says to me.

"What is it dear?" I ask.

"Seeing that we will be spending the anniversary at home because of the lockdown. I am thinking that we invite Adanma, Regina and her husband to come and spend the fourteen days lockdown period with us."

I greatly detested that idea.

"Yes Daddy, that would be wonderful," says Nnabuike. "It has been months since I saw Reggy."

"Yes, that's true," Tolu concurs. "I have been speaking to her on the phone. Something is wrong with my Adanwa."

"That would be wonderful," I said, what else could I have said. "All seven of us together under one roof for fourteen days, that would be amazing."

It was indeed torture. Adanma and I barely spoke to each other or saw eye to eye, figuratively and literally speaking. She kept to herself and everybody wondered why the lastborn of the house was withdrawn. The whole situation made me feel ill and I wasn't faking it. I told Adanma's mother my symptoms as she observed me.

"I think you might be pregnant," she says to me.

"Pregnant?! No that's impossible. I can't be."

"I don't understand. Isn't that what you have been praying for? I am not on call but I can take you to the hospital to be tested. I will tell the soldiers that it is a medical emergency."

"It can't be. I can't be pregnant."

"Are you pregnant?" my husband asks. I didn't hear him when he came into the room.

"I believe she is. The signs are obvious."

"Yes!! This is amazing," Vitalis says, as he lifts me up. "This is wonderful news. We have to tell everyone."

"Oh no we don't," I say. This would be the end of my marriage. I am not sure if my husband or Mr. Williams is responsible. Yes, we always used protection but it is not a hundred percent guaranty. "Please let us not jump the gun. We have to be certain before we make such announcement."

"But, but…"

"No buts. My pride is at stake here. If it turns out that I am not pregnant, people will laugh at me."

"But we are not people. We are your family," says my husband.

"Please, when the time is right, I will make the announcement."

"Okay," my husband says, which was a relief to me.

I and Dr. Regina prepared dinner, and it became clear to me that I was indeed pregnant. Certain foods annoyed me. I hope that the baby is my husband's. I have been praying for this for years, but if I run a test and discover that the child belongs to Mr. Williams, I would have to, and it kills me to say this, terminate it, for the sake of my marriage.

"I suspected it when I first arrived," says Dr. Regina, who has been observing me all the while. "You are definitely pregnant."

We served dinner. Adanma was there and as usual kept quiet.

"Adanma what is it?" her mother asked. "You are sweating."

"Maybe she has corona," Tolu said, as a joke to make her laugh.

"No I am fine," Adanma said.

"But you don't look it," her mother said.

"I know just the thing that will cheer you up," Vitalis said. "In a couple of months, you will be having a brother or sister, or maybe both but we are not sure now."

I wanted so bad to tell him to keep quiet but I couldn't. Mr. Williams, judging from the expression on his face, must have gotten the news from his wife. He too could not do anything.

"Who is pregnant?" asked Nnabuike. "Mum are you?"

"No," said Vitalis. "It is my wife. My wife is pregnant."

He thought he spoke good news, but his words were the last drops of water that broke the dam of Adanma's pent-up anger.

"They are cheating on the both of you!!!" screamed Adanma.

"Daddy, your wife is cheating on you with Mummy's husband."

I could no longer keep it in. I had to say it, I had to save my parents from the sham that has been their second marriages. They both looked at me with doubt, but when they looked at their spouses, they saw the undeniable truth on their faces.

"I am sorry Daddy. I am sorry Mummy. I should have told you a long time ago."

My father stood up from his seat, he was irate and looked a bit boggled. He looked at his wife, though he knew that I wouldn't make up such an accusation, he still had to ask.

"Is it true? Have you been cheating on me with him?"

"Yes," answered the headmistress, owning up to her deeds and begged for forgiveness. "Please forgive me."

She went on her knees and grabbed hold of my father's legs. He kicked her off and she fell to the ground and hid her face in shame. Through all these, my mother had been silent but you can see her thoughts flowing freely from her eyes. That evil man was still sitting next to her. My brother Nnabuike took one of the jugs in his hand.

"Drop it," our mother said to him, then she looked at me. And in her sparkling eyes the word betrayal was clearly written.

I never meant to cause them this much pain. I had decided that I would tell them the truth after we had commemorated the loss of the firstborn of the family. But I could no longer keep it in knowing that the headmistress was pregnant, possibly for her lover.

"So the baby could be his?" my father asked his wife.

"No it definitely isn't. We…"

"Oh shut up there!" said my father to my stepfather, or to that man.

Calling him my stepfather placed him on a pedestal next to my father which he clearly wasn't. He belongs to the depths of the abyss where he crawled out of to cause pain to my family. He was the cause of all this, yet there was not a single tear in his eyes.

"Leave my house," my father said to that man.

"But we are in quarantine. The soldiers will punish me."

"I don't care. I said leave!!"

Seeing that facing the soldiers was better than the wrath of my father, that nymphomaniac, that evil man stood to leave. My mother looked at him and it was clear what she was thinking; Why? Why would you cheat on me? My stepmother, or that evil woman I should call her, because she was working in tandem with that evil man to destroy my family, knelt down again in front of my sweet and innocent father.

Seven lives have been ruined that day, or maybe eight considering that the hag is pregnant. Maybe I should have kept my mouth shut, but I would be living a lie and it would only lead to more pain and devastation. Every single day I wished that my parents hadn't divorced. We wouldn't have gotten into this mess that we are in.

My father looks at my mother. My mother looks at my father. And in their eyes, what they were both thinking was clear. For divorcing each other, they wonder, AM I A FOOL?

PART 4

Fidel the infidel

*Inspired by and dedicated to Mr. Tyler Perry's
masterpiece, Acrimony*

It wasn't a rainy day like any other, it rained cats and dogs and a few ducks. Fidel, a pupil of primary five was waiting patiently in his class for his driver to come and pick him up. It was a Friday and he was eager to begin the weekend. He was not alone in the class. Everyone had gone home except for Rae. She was ten years old just like Fidel, but unlike him, she wasn't looking forward to the weekend because it meant that she had no escape from her abusive parents. She sat on her seat and remained quiet, hoping and praying for the rains not to stop. At least when she gets back home she could tell her parents that the rain had prevented her from coming home immediately after school.

Fidel and Rae barely spoke to each other even though they have been in the same class for two years now. Fidel was bored, so he turned to Rae, the girl who always won the most quiet girl in class award, and said;

"Would you like to share my lunch with me?"

Even in the midst of the storm, Rae heard him quite alright but she just wasn't sure that he was speaking to her.

"Would you like to share my lunch with me?" he repeated.

Then she turned towards his direction as slowly as a sloth. She was surprised to see that he was looking at her. Her eyes went round the room to be certain. Seeing the uncertainty in her behaviour, Fidel went to her with his yellow lunch box in his hand. He sat next to her and opened it.

"My father employed a new maid," he said. "She doesn't know that I don't like pear. She added it to my lunch. Please have it, I don't want it to waste."

Unlike Fidel, Rae liked pear, in fact it was her favourite fruit, not that she told him, but he deduced it from the way she ate it with the slices of bread. She was a proud girl and never asked for help. But for some reason she was comfortable showing this side of herself to Fidel, the most brilliant boy in the class. Yes, he was top only among the boys. Because when it came to the class, Rae was the best. Maybe the reason why they barely spoke to each other was the unspoken rivalry between them.

They were closer to each other than before, physically speaking. And yet, have not spoken six sentences to each other. Maybe words didn't need to spoken. A smile here and there, a glance here and there was all they needed to enjoy each others company.

The torrential rain settled quite a bit. It was safe for Rae to start heading home, but she preferred to stay with her new friend. She still could explain to her parents that the rains had hindered her from coming home. They know that she was unlike other children her age who would play, sing and dance in the rain and get home wet.

Fidel was just about to ask her a question when he spotted his father's driver.

"My driver has arrived," he said, but she said nothing in return.

He locked his lunch box and was just about to head for the door when he remembered that he had forgotten something.

"You should come with us so that he can drop you."

She looked at him and in her eyes he saw the answer. She followed him and as they made their way down the corridor they were met by the driver who had an umbrella in his hand.

"Good afternoon sir," Fidel said to the driver while Rae curtsied.

"Apologies Master Fidel, the rain prevented me from coming when you closed."

"I know. Daddy doesn't like anyone driving in the rain." Fidel looked at Rae whose head was down then he turned his gaze to his driver. "We will be dropping her off. Where do you live?" he asked Rae, but she didn't answer.

"What is the name of the area you live in?" the driver asked.

"I live in Huntington Avenue, just close to the stadium."

"I know where Huntington Avenue is," said the driver with a smile on his face. "Come on, let's get going before the rains start again. You know how the rains are this month."

The driver dropped her off. He had offered to take her to her doorstep but she declined. She thanked him and alighted but didn't say a word to Fidel who was waiting to hear her voice. She left and it took every ounce of strength in him not to look back as she walked away.

The weekend came and he had all but forgotten about Rae. He had a new pair of sandals which he wanted to show to his friends in school. So when Monday came, he wore his new sandals with happiness and felt like he was floating because they were soft on his feet. The maid packed his lunch and in it was a pear. He had forgotten to tell her about his dislike for pear. He left for school as gleeful as ever. His driver dropped him off and he walked in a way that his new shoes were noticeable like the flag of The Isle of Man.

He saw his friends in front so he made his way towards them. As he walked he just turned right for a second and was about to face forward again but what he saw caught his attention. It was a smile, but not just any smile, it was Rae's smile. He was transfixed. His friends called him but he didn't or couldn't hear them. All he saw was Rae smiling at him. All it took was a smile and his whole world changed.

Since that day the two became inseparable. They were always chosen to represent the school in competitions. They either came in in first or second place, and till they graduated, Fidel took the first position in class while Rae came in second.

They talked a lot and made plans for the future though they seemed young. Fidel always wanted to pay her a visit during the weekends or on holidays but she gave one excuse after the other. His parents knew about her and had invited her over a couple of times as they returned from inter-school competitions.

Finally, their graduation day came, and luckily for the pair, they had both been accepted to the same secondary school. Fidel and his parents were excited. The ceremony had commenced two hours ago but Rae hadn't arrived.

"Where is Rae?" Fidel asked his class teacher.

"I don't know," he answered. "I thought you knew since you two are close."

The hands of the clock kept turning round and Rae hadn't arrived. Everyone was shocked when the most quiet and second best student in the class wasn't around to accept her prizes, and there was no one from her family to accept them on her behalf. Fidel received three prizes that day but he was unhappy, without Rae by his side he felt incomplete.

"Daddy," he said to his father. "I want us to go and look for Rae. She wasn't present to accept her prizes."

"We have to get home, there is something urgent I need to do."

"But sweetheart," Fidel's mother said. "Can it wait?" it sounded like a question, but it really wasn't.

"Okay, but we will be quick."

"Thank you Daddy."

They got into the car and left. When they got to Huntington Avenue they asked the first person they saw if he knew Rae's family.

"Yes," he answered, but there was a way he said it that told them that he didn't welcome that question. "Just go down the street. Take the junction by your right, the first house you see, that is it."

"Thank you," Fidel's mother said, but he walked away and gave no care whatsoever for her gratitude.

Fidel's father drove as directed. The first house after the junction wasn't hard to miss but when he got there he just wasn't sure that it was the house. It looked dilapidated. *Are you sure this is the place?* Was the thought in everyone's mind but they never asked. Fidel wanted to come out of the car but his father instructed him to remain inside. He rolled down the windows and they caught a whiff of cannabis. It was unmistakeably coming from the house.

"Be careful dear," Fidel's mother said to her husband.

Fidel's father came out and walked towards the house with his right fist subconsciously clenched. Fidel didn't understand what was going on. He didn't know what the smell was, all that he knew was that it smelled bad. He waited patiently in the car with his mother. His heart began to race faster than the clock which made ten minutes feel like hours. His father came out with his shirt a bit torn. He was livid and walked with long strides.

"We are going to the police station," he said to his family as soon as he got into the car.

"What about Rae?" Fidel asked. "Daddy what about Rae? Is she okay?"

His father just looked at him but said nothing, maybe he hoped that Fidel could read the reaction on his face. His wife placed her hand on his shoulder as he put the car in gear and drove off. They didn't go straight to the police station as Fidel thought. Instead, his father drove him home and left almost immediately without giving any explanation. Fidel wanted to leave home and run straight to Rae's home, but he was under the watchful eyes of his elder brothers who had just returned from boarding school.

It was around eight in the night when his parents returned. He had been waiting anxiously and had not touched the food and gifts his family and domestic servants bought for him. His father came to him, bent down so that they could see eye to eye. Then with a calm voice he said;

"Rae is fine. She is with the police now."

"What happened?" he asked, fearing the worse.

His father stood up but said nothing.

"She is fine, that is all you need to know for now," his mother gave a satisfactory answer. "We will tell you more tomorrow."

Fidel couldn't wait for the next day. His eyes were open till the break of dawn. He did all that was required of him and gave no thought of his planned school shopping. He prepared his own breakfast and was waiting patiently at the sitting room for his parents to come and take him to where Rae was.

"Good morning Daddy, good morning Mummy," he greeted his parents, but they knew that it was more than a greeting.

They had their breakfast and a few minutes to ten they were ready.

"Come let's go," Fidel's mother said to him.

They went to the police station but he was asked to remain in the car with his mother. He had a dozen questions in his mind but he reserved them for Rae since his parents were not forthcoming with the answers. His mother was aware of the elephant in the room but thought it best that her husband should address it. Fidel's father returned and before anyone could ask, he said;

"Social services have taken her."

He thought that he had answered the question, but that only made Fidel have more questions. But he kept them to himself, he knew that Rae wouldn't hide anything from him. It took them just a little over an hour to get there. As usual, Fidel waited while his parents went to make enquiries. He was not alone in the waiting room, there were other visitors too. He was appropriately seated at the section meant for adolescents based on the décor of the room. He looked out the window from time to time hoping that he would see Rae but he didn't. He looked out for the umpteenth time hoping, then someone touched him on his shoulder. He looked back and saw that it was Rae. She looked emaciated but happy to see him.

He hugged her tightly. He had never hugged her like this before because she was a developing girl. But she didn't mind.

"What happened?" he asked. "I was so worried."

"I am okay. Your parents came at the right time to save me. Sit down and I will tell you everything."

They sat down close to each other and Rae narrated her ordeal and all that she had been hiding from him for so long. Her parents were drug addicts.

They were able to hide it from their neighbours for quite some time, but three years ago they gave into their addiction and didn't care who knew. They both lost their jobs and turned their house into a den of addicts. Luckily for Rae, her uncle lived just across the road. He took care of her and she stayed with him from time to time until he died in an accident a month ago. From then things got worse for Rae. She hid the abuse she suffered at home that not even the teachers or her best friend Fidel knew about it.

She loved her parents and did whatever they asked of her as long as it was legal. But lately, they have been trying to get her to take hard drugs with them. She refused vehemently. Her mother put her arms around her and held her tightly while her father forced alcohol down her throat. That was when Fidel's father walked it. What he saw was appalling so he struggled with her father. She cried for him to save her. He knew that it would be better for the police to handle this. So he left, and that is how she ended up here.

"I never knew," said Fidel, which sounded like an apology. "I will never let anything like that happen to you again. I promise," he said with tears in his eyes and meant it.

He visited her every week she spent in the children's home before she was assigned to a foster family. But unfortunately, her foster family together with the support from the government, couldn't afford the fees of the private school she and Fidel got admission to. Fidel was saddened by this news and felt hopeless.

During the holidays he visited her and she visited him when she could. And each time he knew that she was unhappy. Her foster family were not nice but they were better than her real parents. He bought gifts for her which she hid because her foster parents seized whatever he gave her and sold it.

"Do you think that what the government pays us to take care of you is enough?" they would tell her.

She didn't fight back. She prayed for time to run fast so that she would turn eighteen and leave them.

Fidel's parents also checked in on her from time to time and bought her some gifts. They never asked, but it was obvious that their son was dating Rae. Her foster parents were always on their best behaviour whenever Fidel's parents visited. They even asked for some things for themselves, covertly of course, using Rae's name.

The years went by and both Fidel and Rae were in their final year in secondary school. As they grew older so did their dreams grow with them. Fidel wanted to become an engineer and Rae wanted to become an oncologist because she was determined as she has told Fidel countless number of times; to find a cure for cancer in all its forms.

"That is a noble dream," he told her.

"And it will become our reality. Trust me."

"I can picture it," said Fidel. "Rae my bae," as he now calls her. "The inventor of the cure for cancer."

"Fidel! Come on lets go. It is our turn," his classmate said.

Fidel and Rae were representing their schools in a mathematics competition. He has been here a couple of times and his school has always come in second because of one guy - his ultimate rival. This was Rae's first time and it was the first time her school qualified to this stage.

As the competition progressed, three teams or three schools remained to be precise, that of Rae, Fidel and his rival. The questions this time were tougher as it was the final. Fidel's school was in the lead with fifteen points and Rae's school was behind with twenty points. Fidel was not necessarily happy because his school was leading, but because they were ahead of his rival.

As time went on, the other school caught up and surpassed Fidel's school. At the end, the difference between first and second place was just a point. And for the umpteenth time, Fidel's school came in second. Coming second is not bad, but coming second every time when you are this close to clinching the first prize is annoying. But they accepted their prize with feigned grace. Rae's school on the other hand were very content in third place. If you saw them celebrating you would think that they came in first place.

Fidel and his teammates retreated to their school bus where they hid their trophy in shame. When he was done wallowing, he thought he should go and find Rae and congratulate her. He searched and asked her schoolmates if they had seen her but no one had. He continued his search until he found her, sitting in close proximity to his arch rival and giggling. Quickly, he made his way to them.

"Rae," he called, trying his best to cover the anger he felt boiling within. "We need to go."

"Go? Where to?" asked the rival. "Is she your sister or your girlfriend?"

Fidel gave him a stern look with the answer written all over his face.

"I am his girlfriend," Rae answered, to make it clear if there was any confusion that they are in a relationship.

"This guy? You deserve better," said the rival.

It took the calm touch of Rae for Fidel not to punch his rival.

"Let's go," Rae said to Fidel who grudgingly turned and walked away.

They found a quiet place so that they could talk.

"What were you doing with him?" Fidel asked, trying as much as possible not to raise his voice.

"Don't shout at me."

"I did not shout."

"Yes you did."

"No I didn't."

"Yes you did."

"No I didn't!!" shouted Fidel, then he looked at his bae sheepishly.

She left without saying a word. They have had fights before, but this one was different. They didn't speak a word to each other till the term came to an end. Fidel went to visit her with a heart full of apologies, but none was needed, as time has made them realise that they missed each other more than they were angry with each other.

The two lovebirds were happy for a while until tragedy stroke. Fidel's parents died in an automobile accident. He and his two brothers were devastated when they heard the news. It became unbearable for him when he saw their burnt bodies. He ran out of the morgue and went straight to see Rae.

"My parents are dead," he said to her before she could ask why he was crying.

She embraced him and they both cried. Her foster parents didn't allow boys in the house this time of the night, but they made an exception when they heard what happened. Fidel spent the night with Rae in her room as the other foster children left them alone.

He was not the same person in the weeks that followed. He barely spoke to anyone and emaciated to two-third of his former weight, not even Rae his bae could make him eat like he used to. It was until after the funeral that a little light came into his eyes and vigour in his steps. Rae never left his side the whole time. One night when they were alone, Fidel turned to her and said;

"Rae, you are now my family. Everything I am and everything I have is yours. I think we should get married."

Maybe it was his loss talking, but there was no single doubt in her mind that he loved her, and she too loved him. So she said;

"Yes, I will marry you."

Fidel shared the news with his elder brothers. They were happy but thought that it was premature considering that they were still in secondary school.

"I don't think it really matters when two people love each other," Fidel told them. "We will get married when we turn eighteen."

"And how will you take care of yourselves?" asked his eldest brother.

"With his part of the inheritance," answered the second brother who thought that the answer was obvious.

"I will advise that you wait till maybe when you are twenty five. I am twenty six and I am not thinking of marriage."

After much thought, Fidel took the advice of his brother much to the chagrin of Rae.

Fidel applied to and gained admission into the most prestigious college of engineering. The only problem was that it was in another continent so he had to leave his Rae behind.

"Don't forget me," she said to him, with tears in her eyes.

"How can I forget to breathe?" he asked her. "Even when I am sleeping I am always thinking of you. I won't be there forever. I will come back at the end of my second year."

"But that is too long. I want you to school here."

"It was one of my father's wish and prayer that I school in his alma mater. I have to honour that."

Rae didn't know what to say after that. Fidel thought to cheer her up so he said;

"We will get married when I come back."

For a brief moment she was not sad. She hugged him with joy in her heart but then she thought about how much she would miss him. She held him tighter and used every ounce of strength in her being not to tell him to stay.

Two months later, Fidel travelled. He rented an apartment for her to stay now that she was eighteen and an adult legally responsible for herself. She had applied to many schools and had gotten accepted into most of them. But she was not interested in them. She wanted Dobson School of Medicine because it had the best oncology program and carried out hundreds of researches on cancer. They were very selective but wise enough not to let an intelligent girl like Rae slip through their fingers. So one day as Rae checked her mail, she saw her letter of acceptance into the college of her choice.

Fidel was the first person she called. He had indeed become family to her though they were not yet married. Fidel was happy to hear the news which he had prayed and prepared for. He had gotten two jobs and had saved some money. Together with part of his inheritance, he was able to pay for her first year's fee. He sent money from time to time for her upkeep. He wanted her not to be distracted by anything but to focus on achieving her dream - To cure cancer.

At the end of his first year, he decided to surprise her. He had been secretly making wedding plans with his brothers. The one year he spent away from her was torture. So immediately after he landed, he went straight to the apartment he rented for them with his luggage which contained gifts and a ring in his pocket.

He was beaming all the way. He hadn't felt this happy in a long time. He told himself that this was a day he would never forget, and indeed, he never did. He knocked on the door but there was no answer so he walked round the house and peeped through the window. He thought of calling her but he didn't want to ruin the surprise.

One of her neighbours came out believing he was an intruder. He had never seen her before, but as soon as she saw his face she said;

"You are Fidel aren't you?"

"Yes I am. How do you know my name?"

"Your picture is everywhere in the house."

"Please where is Rae? I want to surprise her."

"Well she… she… she is at number 4 Griffiths street," she said briskly.

"Okay, let me go and surprise her. Please can I keep my luggage with you?"

She nodded her head though it felt like she wanted to say something else.

"Thank you," said Fidel.

He followed her to her house where he kept his bags then off he went to see Rae his bae. The taxi ride was faster than he had imagined. He paid his fare then began to make his way with a joyous gait to his steps. He was a couple of feet away from the house when he stopped. What he saw shook him to his very core. It was like breath was taken out of him. He could breathe quite alright but he didn't feel alive. Because in front of him was his Rae kissing his ultimate rival.

"I will miss you," he heard her say to him.

"You can spend another night with me."

"No, I don't want to."

"Please, please," he said, as he tickled her.

She began to laugh and tried to walk away from him and that was when she saw the devastated Fidel standing there, betrayed and heartbroken. He had tears in his eyes. He wanted to speak, but what on earth could he say that would make him feel better.

"Fidel please, I am sorry," Rae pleaded as she went on her knees and joined her palms in supplication.

A ghost he was, figuratively speaking. Fidel began to walk away. She went after him but remained at a distance because she didn't know how he would react if she came close or touched him. He hailed a taxi and asked the driver to take him to his eldest brother's house.

"I am sorry Fidel," his brother said to him after he narrated his ordeal. "What happened isn't right. It is good that you didn't marry her. She doesn't deserve your love. She…"

Fidel knew that his brother was right, but his voice had faded into the background because all Fidel could think about was the horrible sight he saw.

"I need to leave," he said.

"Where are you going?" asked his brother.

"Somewhere… Anywhere… I don't know. I just need to clear my head."

He took the keys to the car that was once his mother's and drove out. He felt hurt and betrayed and wanted that feeling to go away even if it is just for the night. He drove to the side of town notorious for its nightwalkers. He parked his car some metres away from the bevy of cocottes and watched them. Their wigs were a spectrum of colours. It would be difficult to recognise them with their natural hair when they are not working.

Fidel remained in his car with the engine still on. Now that he was here he wondered why he came here in the first place. He put his hands on the steering wheel and began to make a U-turn then his car was hit by a semi-truck.

He woke up three days later in the hospital. His right arm and left leg for heavily bandaged. He tried to move but his neck hurt. He knew quite alright that he was in the hospital, he just didn't know how he got here and why. He looked round the room and was just about to call for a nurse when the door opened. It was Rae. She walked in with tears in her eyes. Maybe they were tears of joy because he had woken up or maybe they were tears of sadness because of her betrayal, but it was hard to say. Fidel on the other hand was very happy to see her and his face brightened with a smile.

She ran to his bedside, knelt down and began to cry. Fidel wondered why she did that, but then his memory came back to him and he remembered how she had betrayed him. He welled up in anger. He wanted to chase her out but then he remembered how she looked to him a second ago. He saw her the way he had always seen her before his return. It is funny how someone could look like an angel one minute and the devil the next. Yes I know, the devil is also an angel but you get my point.

"Leave," Fidel said, which was barely audible because his throat was a bit bruised. "Leave," he repeated, this time a bit louder.

Rae heard him quite alright, but she chose not to leave, she chose not to leave his side again. She had been in the hospital ever since she learnt from the neighbour of Fidel's brother that he was in an accident. She truly felt like her whole world had ended. He truly meant everything to her, and she loathed herself for cheating on him.

Fidel's brothers walked into the room and they found the sight of her kneeling and apologising very appalling.

"What are you doing here?" asked Fidel's immediate elder brother. "I thought we had warned you not to come here again."

Rae stood up, sweating profusely.

"I am truly sorry," she said, it wasn't clear if she was speaking to the brothers or to Fidel because she covered her face in shame. She walked out of the room still crying. The nurses had been told not to let her in, but they did anyway because they felt that it was good for someone to watch over him when they attended to other patients.

Fidel watched as she walked away. Part of him wanted her to stay. She was the light of his world, but now it felt more like scorching heat than warmth. A week later, Fidel was discharged. It would be a long road to recovery so he differed a semester.

Everyday, Rae came over with a cooked meal for him. Fidel's brother never granted her access and had warned her to stop coming. She would drop the food on their doorsteps and the next day she would come to find it still there. But she never gave up. She had to tell him how sorry she was, she had lost the fidelity he had in her but she was determined to get her Fidel back.

Two months later, Fidel's eldest brother had to travel to another state due to work. He hired two aids, a male and a female to assist Fidel. Their middle brother came to take Fidel to the hospital and other things. This was the opportunity Rae had been waiting for and she seized it. One day when Fidel was taking a walk as he called it even though he was limping on one leg. Rae walked into the compound. She was happy to see him hale and hearty. He was shocked to see her, but mostly, he was happy. He turned the other direction and began to limp back to the house.

"Fidel, please wait. Please don't turn your back on me," she said.

He was still very angry with her, but he couldn't bear to cause her pain. So he stopped and turned to face her. On his face was written all the questions she came to answer. And so she began.

"Fidel please forgive me. I was a fool (she began to cry at this moment). I am sorry that I betrayed your trust. I am sorry that I betrayed our love. I never should have done what I did."

"Then why did you do it?" asked Fidel. He fought back tears because men don't cry, or maybe they do, just not in front of women.

"I will not lie to you Fidel. After you left, I felt lonely. There was no one there to comfort me. He knew that I was vulnerable so he started giving me his attention of which it sickens me to tell you that I wanted it to take away my loneliness. One thing led to another and, and…" she couldn't bear to say those words in front of Fidel. And Fidel couldn't bear to have her say it or to hear it himself. The images of them that day still traumatised him.

A few seconds went by with neither of them saying a word, which made Fidel believe that it was his time to speak.

"How can I trust you again? I will still go back to continue my studies. How sure am I that you wouldn't continue with whatever it is that you two had?"

"I have left the school," Rae said briskly. It seems she had been waiting for him to ask that question. "I have transferred to the state-owned university. I will never see him again."

"But the state university's oncology program isn't as good as that of Dobson."

"I don't care, your love and trust is more important to me. I love you and I want to spend my life with you."

Doubtful, Fidel wanted to say. But he saw in her eyes that she meant it.

He looked back at the time he had seen her in the hospital. He had forgotten her transgressions and his spirit lightened at the sight of her. He wanted to have that feeling again, and it was only possible if he could forgive and forget.

He said nothing else that day. He just went back into the house and continued his exercise. Rae continued with her visits, and little by little she began to make her way through the house; from the front door to the sitting room, to the kitchen then to Fidel's room. Little by little she began to make her way back into Fidel's life; from cooking for him, to taking care of him and his injuries, then finally to his heart. It was easier for Fidel not to remember what she did, though his brothers constantly reminded him and told him not to let her back into his life.

"She will do it again," they said. "Women like that can't be trusted."

Fidel prayed and hoped they weren't right because he believed her as she said;

"I will never do it again."

Fidel's brothers got married and she wasn't invited. A week before Fidel went back to school, he and Rae, in a simple ceremony, got married, his brothers refused to attend. She was his wife, and he was her husband, for better, thought Fidel, hoping that the worse was behind them.

It was torture being apart in two different continents. Fidel wanted Rae his bae and wife to come and join him on holidays but it was very expensive. He sent money he earned from his jobs to Rae to pay for her schooling and upkeep. He was determined to see her dream come to fruition. "My wife will discover the cure for cancer," he would tell anyone who asked about his wife. It was a good dream, but very expensive. Fidel barely ate. He focussed mostly on Rae's dreams which were his as well and his studies. At the end, it was worth it. He got offered a good job in his country upon graduation.

Rae was waiting for him when he arrived at the airport. It had been three years since they last saw each other but the moment they hugged each other, it was like no time had passed at all and they continued from where they left off - their honeymoon.

"I missed you so much," said Fidel.

"I missed you too," said Rae.

She noticed that Fidel was much slimmer but she pushed it aside. She was happy to have him back in his arms.

"Where are my brothers?" he asked.

He got his answer from Rae's silence; they still were not on good terms. A fantastic meal as she called it, was waiting for him at home. For two whole weeks, they didn't leave their house except for when Rae went to school. As their honeymoon phase was coming to an end, it was time to address the issue they have been arguing about for years - children. Fidel wanted them now, but Rae wanted to wait.

"We will have all the children we want," she said. "But I want to use this time to complete my work. The results of my tests and trials are positive. I am this close, this close," she said, as she indicated with the little distance between her thumb and index finger, of which Fidel thought hadn't gotten any closer in the passed years.

"Please dear, give me some time. Once I achieve this, all our children and their children's children, and their children's children could retire even though they have not been born. We will be unimaginably rich. You must resign."

"Must?" asked Fidel.

"Yes you must. I too will resign because we would go round the world with our children. We could have as many children as we want. All I ask is for a little patience, just a little patience."

Fidel loved the dream she had, but what he wanted wasn't the money or the cars, the trips or the houses, no. What he wanted was her happiness. He had never seen her light-up like when she talks about her dream. He didn't want to take that away from her, he didn't want to rob or deny her soul.

Years went by and the distance between her two fingers hadn't gotten any closer. Fidel was earning a lot of money but they lived a simple life because all he earned went into his wife's research. It was difficult getting donors. Many people and organisations have donated to the cause and to more established institutions and renowned oncologists. They found it difficult to believe that a young lady like her could find a cure for cancer in all it's forms and stages even though she came out top of her class.

One day, Fidel returned home from work and said;

"Rae bae."

"What is it?" she asked, sensing the excitement in his voice.

"My firm has been offered a contract to construct a nuclear plant and I was chosen as the lead engineer."

"That is good news."

"The pay is wonderful and we could use it to complete the final step of your tests."

"Yes, that would be wonderful. But you will have to be careful with all that radiation."

"Of course I will."

"When do you start?"

"That is it."

"What is it?"

"The job is three states away and I leave next week."

"Three states away?" said Rae, as she stood up. "For how long will you be gone?"

"That is it, since I am the lead, I have to be on site all the time to supervise and make sure that everything goes according to plan. But I promise you I will fly back to you as soon as possible."

Fidel was afraid that the past would repeat itself, but he had to trust his wife. So he left. Things didn't happen as he planned, the work progressed slowly which meant that he had to stay longer than expected. He and Rae communicated often on the phone and one day he had a call that would change his life forever.

"Fidel," Rae said. "I have found it."

"Found what?" he asked.

"I have found the cure."

"Really?"

"Yes, I just need to prove the theory, but it works, it works."

"How do you mean?"

"I need to buy some equipment and the money you gave me isn't enough."

"But I just sent you money last week."

Fidel was angry because lately Rae has been demanding for a lot of money.

"Fidel believe me. If I have this money, in less than a week I will develop a cure."

"How much do you need?" he asked, and she told him, it was quite a hefty sum.

"A week you say."

"Yes."

Fidel thought, but not long and hard about what Rae said. She was his wife and he wanted to make her happy. So against his better judgement, he dipped his hands into the company's coffers and took out the sum Rae needed.

"The contract is moving slow anyway," he said to himself. "In three or four weeks I will return it from the money Rae would make from her cure."

A week went by, then two, and he hasn't heard a single word from Rae. He called her phone but she didn't answer. He called the house and there was still no response. He asked his brothers and they checked up on her but no one knew where she was or had seen her in the last couple of days. Fidel was worried and requested for permission to head back home which was denied because they were at a critical part of construction. But that changed when he slumped on site.

He was rushed to the hospital, and there he remained for three days as the doctors ran different kinds of tests to ascertain what was wrong with him. He had greatly emaciated and lacked physical strength, but that was not his problem. His worry was on his wife, no one has seen her still.

He requested that he be taken home, and his doctor and company agreed. His file was sent to his doctor back home. His immediate elder brother picked him up from the airport, and the first thing he asked was;

"Has anyone seen Rae?"

"No we haven't. But we are searching everywhere."

"We need to report her missing to the police," suggested Fidel.

His brother said nothing because they both were suspecting the same thing; that she has eloped with her lover.

"I am taking you straight to the hospital," his brother said, and it wasn't a suggestion.

After checking his vitals, the doctor admitted him.

"He is not going home," the doctor said. "I received your medical file yesterday and have gone through it. There is something I am suspecting."

"What is it?" Fidel's brothers asked at the same time.

"Let's test for cancer."

"Cancer?" asked the brothers.

Fidel was too weak to speak.

"Prostate cancer to be precise."

"Run the test," said the middle brother.

And the doctor did which confirmed his suspicion. Fidel was devastated by the news. His wife should be here, she was the oncologist of the family. Where on earth could she be? He wondered, as he feared the worse. But his ultimate fear went away when he saw that his ultimate rival was one of the doctors assigned to his case. Rae clearly didn't elope with him, he thought to himself. But this raised a whole bunch of other questions.

"I don't want him on my case," Fidel said to his doctor.

"Why?"

"I just don't want him okay."

"Fine, I will get someone else," said the doctor, then he left.

Fidel's eldest brother walked into the room. Clearly there was something bothering him but he just haven't found the words to say it.

"What is it?" Fidel asked.

"We have found Rae," he answered, but that was not all he had to say. "We went back to her old neighbourhood and found her in a crack den."

"No, that is not true," said a discombobulated Fidel.

But the silence that followed told him that his brother wasn't fibbing. This explained many things; why she requested for that huge sum of money. It wasn't for her cancer research, but to buy more drugs and feed her addiction. She had become like her parents.

Two days later, Rae came to the hospital. She had learnt about his diagnosis and was ashamed of her actions and has decided to clean up her act. It was obvious that she was in withdrawal but the security and nurses let her in because they were colleagues. Fidel almost didn't recognise her. She recognised him quite alright though he was a third of his former weight. She now realised the obvious signs that she had missed.

"I will get you out of this," were the first words she said, because it seems like it was the most important thing at the moment.

Fidel said nothing in return and watched as she took his chart. Where was she all this while when she could have been here helping me? He wondered.

"No, they can't do this," Rae said.

Do what? Fidel wanted to ask, but he kept quiet instead. Just then the doctor came into the room.

"You can't take out my husband's testicles," she said to the doctor.

"That is not our prognosis," he said. "We are yet to make one."

"But that is where you are going with this," Rae said, as she hands him the chart.

"We are not there yet. We need to run a few more tests to ascertain the best course of treatment."

"Does that mean that I can't have children?" asked Fidel, as he sat upright.

"There are ways to go about this if that is the form of treatment we agree on."

"We will get through this Fidel," his wife said to him.

In the weeks that followed, Rae was relentless in finding a cure for her husband. She had lost months of research due to her recent delve into the world of hard drugs. People advised her to go to rehab but she knew that she wouldn't relapse, her husband's health was reason enough for her to be clean.

She and Fidel were not actually on speaking terms. She explained that she had a desire to reconnect with her parents when he was gone. And by so doing, she got into their world and one thing led to the other and she lost control. But now she was back to her former self and was determined to save her husband's life and secure their chances of having children.

"The cancer is hormone-sensitive," the doctor said, confirming Rae's earlier prognosis. "We would have to remove both testes to reduce the level of testosterone in your body for you to survive. If we don't you have about six months to live. We can bank your sperm so that you can have children later."

Rae and Fidel had already discussed this option if she wasn't able to come up with a cure in time. There was still hope, Fidel thought. But Rae was disappointed in herself. She was this close to completing her work. She could feel it. If only they had more time, but most importantly, if she hadn't squandered the money Fidel sent to her.

Both the sperm deposition and surgery were successful. Fidel's brothers wanted him to stay with them as he recovers but he wanted to go back home with his wife. Everything Rae did told him that she was sorry for her recent escapades with drugs, words were just not enough. Fidel saw her effort and the sincerity in her eyes, so he let her win back his trust one day at a time.

When they were back home and settled, Rae sat next to Fidel on their bed and said;

"I want us to start a family now."

"What?"

"I would like to complete my work but some things are more important and it took me almost losing you to figure that out."

"You are serious."

"Yes, my work can wait. You are my life and I want us to have our children now. As soon as I give birth to our first child I will rest for five months then we would try again."

They had three straws of Fidel's sperm, which means that they had three attempts. Rae was confident that all tries will be successful. This brought happiness to Fidel, he really wanted to hear something good at this time in his life. So they began to make plans. Rae had a well-equipped lab at home where she worked on her cure. She was going to retrieve the samples from the hospital and store them then inseminate herself when the time came.

"They are capable," she told her husband. "But I have heard cases where samples were switched and people ended up raising other people's children. It was a lengthy court battle of which there was no precedence or laws written for such an occurrence."

Fidel agreed with her and so they made their plans and marked dates on the calendar when she would inseminate herself and possible dates of delivery. They had been through a lot but this was the happiest either of them have been of late. So when the day came, which they believed was the start of their new life, and indeed it was. Rae set out to the hospital to retrieve the samples. Fidel was home alone, waiting, then he heard a knock at the door. He peered through the window and saw that it was two of his colleagues. They must have come to check up on me, he thought, and he was right, partly.

"Please come in," he said, with a smile. "Come in."

He offered them drinks but they declined and went straight to business.

"Fidel," one of them said. "The company is concerned about your health but that is not the major reason we are here today."

"Then what is it?"

"We discovered that you took a huge chunk of the money that was given to you to build the nuclear plant. Normally we wouldn't worry because we trust you, but the funds are unaccounted for and the work is lagging behind. So we have come to ask you what you did with the money."

Fidel battled with telling them the whole truth, but then he decided to only tell them parts of it.

"I used it," he said. "And I will pay back as soon as possible."

"Thank you for your honesty Fidel," said the second man, who was the senior colleague. He stood up, looked at the other man which signalled him to get on his feet too. "Expect your letter of termination tomorrow," he said. "The company understands the condition you are in and will not file criminal charges against you. They will however, deliberate on your case and determine how long you will have to pay back what you stole. Any failure on your part will incur the full weight of the law. Have a nice day Mr. Fidel."

They left. Fidel was hit hard by this news though he had been expecting it. He has lost his job now that he was planning on starting a family. He couldn't eat and he didn't call Rae because he didn't know what to say to her. He decided to take a walk, maybe that would help ease his pain.

Rae on the other hand was having problem in the fertility arm of the hospital. As she had suspected, they had problem locating Fidel's samples. The nurse on duty has been going up and down checking both files on shelves and in the computer. Rae had gone on a few errands to get some household stuff and planned on getting to the hospital at 6pm when the next shift starts so that whoever she met wasn't fatigued but as active as an intern trying to prove him or herself. But her calculations were wrong. It took over three hours for the container to be found with the exact serial number, name, date of collection and the number of straws in it.

"I am highly disappointed in you," Rae said to the nurse. "What kind of service do you render here?"

She tried to collect the container from the nurse who hesitated a bit before she let it go. Angry, Rae went back to her car but things only got worse. The car refused to start. She tried and tried but still got the same result. She was stranded, taxis were not near or easy to come by at this time of the night. She had a long walk or if someone could assist her, that would be nice.

"I noticed that you are having problems with your car," Rae heard someone behind her say.

She turned and to her shock, it was Fidel's ultimate rival. She didn't know what to say to him as she has promised her husband that she would never see or speak to him again. Which she has.

"I can give you a lift," he offered.

"No, thank you," Rae said.

"Oh come on. What happened between us is in the past. I mean no harm, I just want to help. It will be unchivalrous of me to just drive away and leave you stranded."

Rae honestly didn't want to get into his car, but she knew that the samples lose their virility the longer they spend outside a tank of liquid nitrogen. So she got in. No word was said throughout the journey. Rae was surprised to see that he still remembered the road to her house. She had no intention of letting him drop her in front of her house. It would raise unnecessary questions and cause trouble in her marriage.

"Drop me by that junction there," she said.

"No," said Fidel's rival. "Your house is just by the corner. I will drop you off there."

"I said no, drop me here," said Rae, as she grabbed the wheel and turned it towards the curb but it went further.

"Okay," Fidel's rival said, as he brought the car to a stop in the middle of the road. "I will…"

He was distracted for only a couple of seconds, but that was all it took for them not to notice an oncoming vehicle. It was coming in full speed and crashed into them. Their car tumbled a couple of times but luckily for them, they had on their seatbelts. They were dazed and concussed, wounded but still alive.

"Are you alright?" asked Fidel's rival when he came to.

"Where is… where is…"

"Where is what?"

"Where is my husband's sample?"

"What?"

Rae began to look through the wreckage. The car landed upright but she couldn't find Fidel's sperm sample. She unfastened her seatbelt and began to look around. She was in pains but she didn't care.

"Someone has come to help us," Fidel's rival said. "He is helping the other driver." He unfastened his seatbelt but could barely move. "Help! Help! Rae we are saved."

Rae didn't care, if she had broken a rib or two, or even a leg, that would be fine. What she wanted more than anything in the world was for her husband's samples to be fine. But unfortunately, she felt a cold sensation on the carpet and traced it to the side of a seat and then she saw the container, open and the samples destroyed. Her whole world sank underneath her. She picked the straws and tried, though she knew it was pointless, to save them.

"He is coming to save us," Fidel's rival said as he noticed the silhouette of their rescuer coming towards them. "This door is damaged," he said to their rescuer. "Use the other door."

Rae was in tears and still had the damaged samples in her hands when the door opened. She looked at the man who had come to rescue them, and to the surprise of both of them, they were each others spouse. Fidel saw what was in her hands. He too felt like the world had disappeared under his feet. But he had to face reality, he had to focus on what was more important at the moment, and that was saving his wife. He was just about to take her out of the car when he saw that the driver was his ultimate rival. He was taken aback. How possible is it for one person to lose everything he has in one day? He thought to himself.

He had lost his job; his chances of having children have been destroyed; but worse of all, his wife was cheating on him again, he thought. Reading the reaction on his face, Rae wanted to explain what had happened but Fidel left. She came down from the car and went after him. They both walked slowly, Rae due to her injuries and Fidel due to his broken soul.

"Fidel please wait," pleaded Rae. "I can explain everything. It is not what…"

Fidel stopped then turned back and faced her.

"What have I ever done to you to make you hurt me like this?"

"It is not…"

"My brothers were right. I have been a fool all these years believing that you have changed."

"Fidel, Fidel…"

"You have ruined my life. I curse the day that I met you. I should have left you alone that day in class. I want a divorce."

"Fidel, I can explain," Rae said, but Fidel didn't care what she had to say.

He walked away just as they heard the sound of an ambulance. Rae went back and was taken to hospital. She spent the night there and returned to a Fideless home the next morning. She called but he never picked. She visited his brother's house but was never allowed to see him. She persisted, insisting that she was innocent and hoping for a reconciliation, but her hope died when she was served with divorce papers.

Life without Fidel was torturous. It was almost unbearable as she watched his brothers come and take his personal items. Many times she had the urge to go back to drugs, but fought it because of her love for Fidel and the promise she made to him. She dreaded the idea of being divorced from him but was excited because she was going to see him for the first time in three months in the office of his divorce lawyer.

"All my client wants from you is to sign the divorce papers. The house and its contents belong to you."

They have been in this office for over an hour, and throughout that time, Fidel never spoke a word to her.

"Fidel," she said, then he looked at her for the first time. "I didn't cheat on you, believe me. You are my life and I will never hurt you like that again."

She hoped that her final plea would make him reconsider. She looked in his eyes and saw a glimmer of hope, but alas, it was just it. Fidel looked away.

"Please don't leave me. If you stop believing in me there is nothing I have left."

She waited for a few seconds, but then she realised that she was only prolonging the inevitable. So she signed it, she signed her divorce papers.

Life without Rae his bae was torturous. It was like learning how to walk again. He didn't go out on dates and hasn't been able to secure employment in the passed six months because of the reason of his termination from his former work. He was just sitting alone in the apartment his brothers rented for him when he got a call for a job interview in a prestigious engineering firm he didn't apply to.

"Are you sure you have the right Fidel?"

"Yes," said the caller. "Your interview is by nine. Don't be late."

Fidel was still sceptical but he went regardless. It wasn't an interview per se but an employment. He was appointed as the head of a department with full benefits and a handsome salary, better than what he was paid at his former job.

"Why me?" he asked the managing director.

"You have a mysterious benefactor."

He started work immediately.

The first weekend after he started his new job, he heard a knock at the door then he went to open it. To his surprise, it was Rae.

"Rae," he said.

"Please may I come in?" she asked with a smile on her face.

He didn't say a word and let his gestures do the talking. He didn't know if to offer her a seat or not. He was still angry with her, but at the same time he was still happy to see her.

"I have found it," she said,

"Found what?" he asked.

"I have found the cure for cancer."

"You have?" asked Fidel, as a voice in his head said, 'I knew she would do it'.

"Yes. You are the first person I wanted to share the news with as soon as I cracked it. But because of our relationship I had to hold on till now."

"I am so proud of you. I always knew that you would do it."

"Thank you Fidel. To show my appreciation," she puts her right hand into her purse and brings out a cheque. "I have this for you." She hands him the cheque.

He looks at the figure and was shocked.

"Are you serious? Are you that wealthy to give me this amount?"

Rae smiled.

"I told you that…" she stopped what she was saying as she was about to broach a subject she vowed she wouldn't. "Well I just came to give you this and to say thank you."

"For what?"

"Everything."

She turned and began to leave. She was at the door when Fidel asked;

"Are you my mysterious benefactor? Are you the one who got me my job?"

"Yes," she answered, but didn't look back, then she walked away.

Fidel didn't know what to say as he stared at the cheque. It was a hundred times more than what he owed his former company. If he wanted he could resign from his new job, share the money with his brothers and their children would be taken care of for life. He shared the news with his brothers and they were elated to hear it and were amazed that Rae was that rich. Their perfect wives were happy too and wanted their share of the money like they had contributed in any way. This caused a stir in their perfect marriage, if any marriage can be called that.

The news of Rae's success filled the news both nationally and internationally. She was called a genius, everyone wanted to associate with her - the doctor who found the cure for cancer. Orders were coming in from near and far, her name would live for eternity. Fidel was proud of her though he wasn't there by her side as he had always imagined.

His was reading an article about Rae his former bae one Saturday in his apartment when he heard a knock at the door. He went and opened it. It was a woman, he didn't recognise her but she knew him.

"Please sir, may I come in?" she asked.

Fidel invited her in. He offered her a seat but she declined. He was about to ask the reason for her visit when she began to cry.

"Mr. Fidel, please forgive me."

"I don't understand. What have you done that you need my forgiveness?"

"I am a nurse. I am a nurse in the hospital where you stored your sperm samples."

"Okay," said Fidel, not knowing where this was going.

"I made a mistake. I am the reason why you divorced your wife."

Fidel began to laugh, "My wife is the reason why I divorced her not you."

"Sir, it truly was my fault. I had not been working long at the bank when I was asked to store your sample. I mishandled it and destroyed the sample, and for that I am truly sorry."

"No you didn't. It was destroyed during the accident."

"No sir, it was destroyed before then, that was why I was afraid to give it to Dr. Rae when she requested for it."

Fidel who was standing, found a chair and sat on it.

"I don't understand what you are saying."

"I was going to resign and confess the next day but then I saw your wife in the hospital and learnt from a fellow nurse that the samples were destroyed in an accident and she blamed herself."

Fidel stood up again.

"Are you saying… are you saying…" he found it difficult to come to terms with the truth she just revealed.

"I thought I was cleared and let her take the blame. But over the months I haven't been able to live with myself, especially now that she has invented a cure that has saved the life of my child. I am overwhelmed with guilt and I hope that I could make things right for you two again."

Fidel sat back down. Deep down, he believed Rae when she said nothing happened between her and his rival. But that day was a difficult day for him. He didn't act irrationally, he just wanted the pain to stop, and he believed that ending his marriage with Rae would put an end to it. If he knew what he knows now, maybe he wouldn't have asked Rae for a divorce.

"Can you please just go," he said to the nurse. He was barely audible but she got the message.

A barrage of thoughts and emotions went through his mind and body as he recalled that fateful night. He had lost it all, or maybe cruel fate had taken it from him. But then he realised, if it was possible for him to lose it all in one night, then he could get it all back in one day also. So he stood up, determined to take his fate in his own hands, and went to meet Rae.

She was having a press conference in a hotel this afternoon. He knew this because the whole world did and they came to hear her speak. He had to park his car metres away and made his way through the crowd. Luckily, he met one of her friends who took him through security to the hall. He couldn't make his way to the front, so he stayed at the back where he had a good view of the stage.

Rae was there answering questions. The hall was quiet when she spoke because they wanted to hear what this brilliant mind had to say. As soon as this press conference is over, I will go and meet her, Fidel thought.

"You said in one of your interviews, that during your darkest hour, a knight came and saved you. Who is that knight?" asked a journalist.

"It is darkest before the dawn right?" asked Rae with a smile on her face but she looked sad. "Great moments in history and great inventions are made at a cost. The inventor or conduit in which they come through bears the weight of everyone living and those unborn on her or his shoulders. They sacrifice a lot to improve on the lives of billions they will never meet.

You see the success but not the pain. If such tales are told, if you could open the curtains and view the lives of these people or the lives of those they came from; you may stop and ask, was it worth it? And the answer you would get is emphatic - For the good of everyone, yes."

Rea paused for a while before she continued her speech. "Well, to answer your question. Yes I had lost everything and had no motivation of carrying on. But then my good friend," she beckoned on him to come and share the stage with her.

Everyone clapped including Fidel, but then he stopped when he discovered that it was his ultimate rival. He climbed on stage and gave Rae a peck on her right cheek. This made Fidel fume with anger. How dare he kiss Rae his bae? He wished he had a gun, he would have killed him right here and now. Or if he could turn back the hands of time he would have killed him before he and Rae met.

"He came to check up on me. I showed him my research. He saw where I was heading but didn't have the money to see it to completion. I actually had the money but I wasted it on frivolous things."

"Are you saying that you would have invented the cure earlier than now?" asked another journalist.

"Yes," answered Rae. "Like I told you, such tales are not as glamorous as you think." She kept quiet for a while as she looked at Fidel's rival. "He took me to the hospital where he worked. They had purchased a new machine which was what I needed so I didn't have to engineer one myself. Not that I could, I had someone years ago who did that for me. It pushed my work months ahead and today here we are, with a cure for cancer."

Everyone in the hall began to clap, everyone but Fidel whose tears was hidden in the back.

"I hear congratulations are in order," said a third journalist.

"Yes," said Fidel's rival as he placed his right hand on Rae's belly.

I can attempt to put it in words, but there are literally no words in any language that has been invented or will ever be invented that can describe how Fidel felt at this very moment as he wondered, AM I A FOOL?

PART 5

The ego of Diego

It is a normal thing to have jitters on your wedding day. But the expression I see on my friend's face, Diego, is more than that. It is like he came alive and realised that he is making a big mistake. He looks at me, and I swear it is like he is a different person. Maybe he is, he had been away in a remote rural area for months. No one knew where he was except for me his best friend.

"Diego, what is wrong?" I ask him.

He finds a chair and sits on it like his knees have gone weak. He still has that look on his face.

"Flavio," he calls me to his side.

"What is it?"

"Mercedes, we have to go and find her."

"Mercedes? Who is that?" I ask. He clearly needs to explain better. "I don't understand. You have to explain. Tell me what is in your mind."

He fights back tears as his eyes went round the room. He breaths heavily and I can't tell if it is from exhaustion or anger. Whatever the problem is he has to tell me. It is about two hours to his wedding, and as typical Spanish weddings go, all his relations and those of the bride are here. He rests his head on his palms and then he begins to narrate his tale from the middle. But for you who are just coming in. I have to start from the very beginning.

Diego and I have been best friends since childhood. I spent a lot of time in his family estate, *Hacienda de Gutierrez*. Our fathers were close and both in the oil business. But unlike my father, Diego's father, Jorge, is into the export of goods and owns a large shipping company. It is safe to say that Jorge Gutierrez was the richest man in the country, which meant that Diego was spoilt rotten.

Unfortunately, he lost his mother when he was three years of age. And soon after that, his father got remarried to unarguably the most beautiful woman in town. Her name is Rosita. There was always an air of mystery surrounding her. She was an amalgamation of rumours. Some say that she is the last surviving heiress of a wealthy family. Some called her a spy, a Mata Hari of sort, who was sent by a rival nation to report on our oil exploration. Others called her *la bruja* because she bewitched the wealthiest man in the country. Whatever the case may be, we all knew not to mess with her.

Diego loved her so much but the feeling wasn't mutual. He didn't remember much of his mother and Rosita made sure of this as she removed all traces of her except for a baby picture of Diego and her during his baptism in a monastery which Diego saved.

Rosita gave birth to a son called Mateo. And like mother like son, he hated Diego. Three years after the birth of her son, Rosita gave birth to another child, a daughter called Maria de la Rosa. She was the light of the house. I should know, I married her.

Diego and I attended the same schools and went to the same university. I studied law and he majored in business administration. He got his MBA soon afterwards. His father was grooming him to take over the family business much to the chagrin of Rosita who wanted that position for her son Mateo.

Diego lived a flamboyant life. He had many people who claimed to be his friends. And he had a lot of girls whom he told were his one and only girlfriend. He was a Casanova like Don Juan DeMarco and very egotistic.

"You know you will get into trouble one day," I told me.

"That, my dear friend Flavio, will never happen," he said, tipsy and with a drink in his hand. "Even if it happens, my father would bail me out."

Maybe it was prophecy but I intended it as a warning. That night, on his way to his hotel room, he and three of his lady friends got into an accident. The ladies were injured while he on the other hand who caused the accident, walked away unscathed. Somehow he found his way home and passed out on the floor of his bedroom.

The next day, the police were at *Hacienda de Gutierrez*. They never come here because of who Jorge Gutierrez is, but on this day, they came with ten squad cars to arrest the errant Diego. His father was just about to go to work when the police arrived.

"How can I help you officers?" asked Jorge.

"We are here to arrest your son Diego," said the arresting officer. "He fled the scene of an accident last night involving the daughter of the governor."

"That can't be true," said Jorge, in shock.

"She is in critical condition but the other girls named Diego as the driver. Where is your son now sir? We have strict orders from the governor to bring him immediately to the station."

"He is passed out in his room," said Mateo, who had been eavesdropping. "You will find him in his own vomit."

"Please lead the way," the officer said to Mateo who was happy to oblige.

My friend was cuffed and was barely awake as the officers dragged him to the police station. His father was dismayed, never had he been disgraced like this. I got to learn all about this in the afternoon when I came visiting. No one told me exactly, I overheard Rosita talking to Mateo.

"Now is our opportunity," the mother said to her son. "Your father has to realise that Diego is not a suitable heir to his fortune. I spoke with the police commissioner and I told him that he shouldn't grant bail to Diego no matter the reason because I want him to learn his lesson."

"But you know that he and Father are close."

"I told your father the same thing and he agreed with me."

I left after this. I tried to visit my friend but I was told that he was prohibited from having any visitors. I wasn't happy but I hoped that Diego would learn his lesson and most importantly, I prayed that the governor's daughter recovers.

A week went by and no word from Diego's family. I returned home one evening after work and found Diego lying on my settee, stinking up the place.

"Diego! Have you been released from jail?"

"No, I am still there. What you see is an apparition."

"I am so glad that you are out. That means that the governor's daughter is well."

"Yes she is. That would be the last time I allow any girl give me any substance while I am driving."

"I think you should go home. Your father must be worried."

"Home? Have you forgotten? *Su casa es mi casa.*"

Diego stayed at my place for a week to allow his father's anger calm down. He chose the time when his father would be at work and snuck in. Rosita and Maria de la Rosa were home.

"Mother look," said an elated Maria de la Rosa. "Diego is back."

She races to the door and hugs her brother. If there was one thing he missed while he was at my place, it was his sister.

"*Buenos dias madre*," he greeted.

"How many times have I told you? I am not *su madre*," Rosita said.

She had indeed corrected or warned him severally but Diego didn't care.

"Where have you been? Father has been worried about you."

"You should have guessed."

"Oh, you were at Flavio's. How is he?"

"He is fine. He sends his regards," he said to his sister, but to her, it meant more than that.

"The maids cleaned your room days ago in anticipation of your return. Come let's go. It is so good to have you back home."

Mateo wasted no time in telling their father that Diego was home as soon as he returned from work. Jorge asked that his wayward son be brought to him in his study. Diego walked in, trying his best to look as remorseful as possible. Once his father set eyes on him, he let his rage loose.

"Do you know what kind of disgrace you have brought to this family?!"

"*Tranquilo papi.*"

"Don't ask me to calm down. Do you know what would have happened to this family if the governor's daughter hadn't recovered?"

"I am sorry father."

"You have said this countless number of times that it has become meaningless. You need to change. You need to become responsible so that you can takeover my business after I retire. But I feel that you will never change. So I have decided to name Mateo my…"

"I will change Father. In fact I have changed. Just give me the opportunity to show you."

Jorge thought long and hard about this, then he said;

"You only have one chance. If you fail me I will…"

"I will not fail you Father, I promise. Santa Maria is my witness."

Diego of course was lying. He just had to pretend long enough for his father to trust him again, then he would go back to his normal ways. The next day, his father took him to Gutierrez Oil and Gas. He had been there on many visits, but today he starts work, officially.

"Father, where are we going? Isn't our office at the top floor?"

His father just laughed and kept on walking to the back of the building. Diego has never been to this side of the establishment before. This must be a tour, he thought. They would start from the down floor then make their way up.

"*Buenos dias* Señor Gutierrez," the housekeeping staff greeted the elder Gutierrez then the younger one.

"Good day all," said Jorge. "Today is my son's first day and he would be starting with you."

"Oh now I get it," said Diego. "I will be supervising them."

"No, not at all. They will be the ones supervising you."

"I don't get it."

"This here is Señor Castillo, the head of housekeeping. He will teach you all you need to know. And when he is satisfied that you have learnt all that is necessary, I will send you to the next department."

"No Dad, you can't be serious. I have an MBA. I did not go to university to become a cleaner."

"In order to run this business, you must have intrinsic knowledge on how every part works."

"No Dad, you can't be serious," said Diego to his father who was walking away.

"Welcome to housekeeping," said Castillo. "I have over twenty years experience in housekeeping. Because you are the boss' son and will one day run the company, I will teach you everything I know. Come, follow me."

Diego could not believe what was happening. During break he called me and told what was happening. I thought it was a joke but he sounded serious. So I left legal and rushed down to housekeeping to find my friend with a mop in his hand. I almost killed myself with laughter.

"This is his way of punishing me," said my good friend. "I went to Harvard business school. I shouldn't be mopping the floor. I am not doing this." He throws the mop away. "I need to see my father."

I followed him and waited outside as he spoke to his father. He came out looking more furious than ever.

"What did he say?" I asked, and I got my answer in his murmuring.

It was the same drama for a week, until one day I told my friend the truth.

"Diego," I said. "You have to put your ego aside. If you want to become the boss one day, you have to play by your father's rules. There is no escaping it as he has made it clear. The longer you refuse, the longer you remain here. And who knows, your father might change his mind and name Mateo his successor."

This time I knew he heard my advice. He ruminated over it for about a week then he began his work in earnest but he made sure to hide his face whenever someone he knows walks by. On the last day of the month, I was waiting for him at the parking lot to give me a ride home because my car was being repaired, but he never came. So I went to look for him. I found him in the housekeepers changing room. He was sitting down, quiet and with a paper in his hands.

"What is the problem Diego?"

"It is my… my…" he grinned. "It is my paycheck," he finally said, with the smile still on his face.

He handed it to me and I saw his pay. It wasn't much, it was less than ten percent of what I made. But he was very happy, in fact happier than I who got paid more. I was happy for him because he was happy.

"So what are you going to do with your first paycheck?"

He thought about it for a while, then the smile on his face widened.

"I know just what to do."

He never told me what it was and I never asked. But I got to know on Sunday after we returned from mass. He had with him a bunch of flowers and a box. Maybe he has found a new lady, I thought. But if he did, I would be the first person he told, so no. I was seated in the sitting room on a settee when I sighted him. The rest of his family with the exception of his father were seated watching a telenovela.

With the flowers and box in his hands, he knelt down before his stepmother Rosita and said;

"I bought this for you mother." He hands her the roses and the box. "I know it is not up to the class or as expensive as the ones you wear. But I bought them with my first salary. I hope you like it."

Rosita opens the box and in it was a necklace and a pair of earrings. Mateo who was sitting next to her took a peek and then he began to laugh.

"Are you serious?" he said. "Do you expect my mother to wear such a cheap necklace?"

"You buy your numerous girlfriends expensive jewellery and this is what you buy for me?" said Rosita, as she closed the box.

"Mum take it. It is something of honour," said my queen Maria de la Rosa. "When has Mateo ever bought anything for you? Diego is the one who remembers you every Mother's Day."

Grudgingly, Rosita accepted the gift and her "Thank you," was anything but a show of gratitude. Diego accepted it anyway. When I was alone with my friend, I asked him this question.

"Why do you keep showing her love when she despises you?"

"I remember little of my mother," Diego answered. "My stepmother is the only mother I know, so I respect her and would shower her with love as I would my mother if she were alive."

"But you should have gotten the hint by now that she doesn't like you."

"That doesn't matter because I love her."

As the months went by, he progressed up the building and made sure that Rosita gets something from his paychecks. He learnt from the various departments but he couldn't learn or be taught everything. I was happy when he came to the legal department. It coincided with the day a new lawyer was hired.

"Hello, my name is Diego," he said, but he didn't introduce himself as the boss' son.

"Nice to meet you," she said. "My name is Alba, Alba de San Martin."

"Nice to meet you too Alba de San Martin," said Diego, to the lady who would be his bride.

They were taught about the legal aspect of the company at the same time. This meant that they spent a lot of time together, and soon afterwards, they began dating and Diego nicknamed her Alba *del Fuego* for reasons he only shared with me. He introduced her to the family and surprisingly, she and Rosita became good friends. It was at this point I decided to confess to Diego that his sister and I are in love. I believe that since he was happy, he could allow me be happy.

"You think that I never knew?" he said, which surprised me. "I knew all along. As a matter of fact, I knew before you two started dating."

"You did? Then why didn't you say anything?"

"I loved playing with you and seeing how you both pretended when people are around. It was quite funny. But the main reason why I said nothing was because I wanted to observe you. I am more like Lothario and you are more like Griselda."

"Griselda? That is the best analogy you could come up with?"

"The male version of her. What I mean is that you are loyal and honest. You are like a brother to me, even more than Mateo. And I am happy that you and Maria de la Rosa have found love and happiness in each other."

"Really?" asked Maria de la Rosa as she came out of hiding. "I told you that he would approve." She hugs me then says to her brother, "So you knew all this while?"

And Diego answered by hugging us both. Things moved quickly and we headed for the altar, not that she was pregnant but because her father insisted. Diego was my best man of course but his dual functions as a brother of the bride meant that he was all over the place.

I will never forget what he told me on our way to church where I would receive the sacrament of Holy Matrimony.

"Ever since Maria de la Rosa's *quinceañera*, I promised myself that she will marry a good man who will love, cherish, respect and honour her. And today, I am happy that I kept that promise, because she is getting married to the best man I know. You are a good man, and I know you will take care of my sister."

No better words could have been said to make me feel happy at that moment. My wedding was the happiest day of my life and I wanted the same for my friend.

"You should think of settling down my friend."

"I am," he said, which surprised me.

"Really?"

"Yes. I am thinking about proposing to Alba."

"I think you should do it. As long as you are certain that is."

"I think I am."

"Then I wish you the best my brother."

After our wedding, Maria de la Rosa and I went on our two weeks honeymoon. And in the two weeks of my absence, a series of events happened that brought us here to the confused state of Diego on his wedding. This is my first time hearing the whole of it and he never told anyone, because he couldn't.

The first thing that happened was that Jorge Gutierrez announced that he would be making his son the next CEO of Gutierrez Oil and Gas and other subsidiary companies. Diego had completed his training and has been deemed worthy by his father to takeover from him. This was a double celebration because he was planning to propose to Alba.

He bought a ring. He didn't plan on taking her out on an expensive date. He had learnt to appreciate the little things in life. Their engagement celebration would come later. He didn't want to take away the feeling of euphoria people still had because of his sister's wedding.

He was going to surprise Alba at her home and he believed she would say yes. He knocked at the door but there was no answer. He tried the knob and it opened.

"Hello, Alba. Where are you?"

She must be sleeping, he thought. So he made his way to the bedroom. He opened the door and walked in, then he saw Alba naked on her bed lying next to a man who was equally naked. He moved back in shock and then he knocked down a lamp and this caused the two lovers to wake up.

"Diego?" the man said.

"*Ay Dios mio*," said Alba, as she covered herself. "I can explain," she said. The only rhetorical statement ever to exist.

Diego was heartbroken and speechless. He wished he could pounce on them and kill them, but of what use would that be. He put the ring back into his pocket and walked away. He thought about going to drink but he had learnt of the repercussions of such an act. So he drove home instead.

"Diego," Jorge called, as soon as Diego walked in.

Diego said nothing but just looked at his father.

"Come with me to my study. There is something I have to discuss with you."

"Father can it wait?" he asked, as he had a lot on his mind.

"No, not today," his father answered.

So Diego followed him.

"*Mijo*, what I am about to tell you is something I should have told you a long time ago. But you should know that it doesn't change anything."

"What do you mean father?" asked Diego as he sat down. He really wasn't ready for another bad news today.

"Just remember, it doesn't change anything," reiterated Jorge. "No one knows this, or maybe they have forgotten. But after your mother and I got married, we had difficulty conceiving. We went to different fertility specialists and they all said one thing, that your mother's womb was inhospitable for a baby."

"I don't understand father," said Diego. He was still holding on to the pain of seeing Alba naked in bed with another man. He wanted to save himself from the hurt that was coming, but he had to stay, he had to hear it all.

"Accepting the truth, your mother and I decided to adopt but we didn't want people to know that we had adopted. We wanted to pass the child as our biological child. So we travelled out of town for months to create the illusion. We went to various orphanages looking to adopt a new-born but we weren't lucky. Until one day, we stopped at a monastery to give some assistance and that was when we heard the news; a woman had abandoned her infant the night before and he was at the orphanage nearby. So we went, and there we met Sr. Rebecca who told us what happened.

She was on her way back from assisting in the hospital when she heard the cries of a woman in pain. She traced the voice into the bushes and found a woman in labour. She was a trained nurse and assisted in the delivery. It was complicated but at the end the child came out safe. The Sister gave the child to the mother and went to the road to get help as she saw headlights approaching. But when she returned, the mother had left but the child was still there. They searched and searched but they never found her. She brought the child to the orphanage and told them this tale that I am telling you now my son."

"So what are you saying Father? Tell me the truth."

"You Diego, are that child."

At this point, Diego stood up from his chair. He couldn't believe that his whole life was a lie. His sense of identity was gone. He couldn't say the words out loud but it was written all over his face - Who am I?

"It was fate my son. God put you in our arms. We talked to the orphanage and they agreed for us to adopt you after three months if the mother wasn't found. We stayed with you everyday. Your mother nursed you like she had given birth to you herself. Three months passed and they gave you our son to us and immediately we had you baptised in the monastery."

"So I am a *bastardo*."

"No you are not. You are my son. Your mother is still your mother."

"My mother abandoned me at birth and I have no father."

"I am your father."

"No you are not! I am a son of no one. I have been told a lie my whole life. I can't be around you anymore."

"Diego please wait," Jorge pleaded, but Diego walked out of the study.

Diego could no longer hold back his tears. He went to his room and cried his soul out. That day was the worst day in his life. His sense of self-worth was tarnished. No one cared for him, no one loved him. This wasn't his home. Maria de la Rosa wasn't his sister. In fact Mateo was the true successor to Jorge not him. He could no longer stay here, he had to leave, not just to get away but to get answers. And the only place he could find these answers was at the place of his birth. He took the picture of his baptism and turned the back. On it was written, in his mother's hand, *Diego's baptism at the Monastery of San Juan, Puebla de Cruz*. Puebla de Cruz was a remote village eight states away. But it didn't matter the distance. Wherever it was Diego would go to find the answers to the question of his identity.

And so, with the money he had on him and the engagement ring still in his pocket, Diego left.

Finally, the wishes of my exes have come true. I have found myself a good man who loves me and treats me right. His name is Diego Gutierrez, *mi vida*. The whole world makes sense when you find your soulmate. The past, present and future all merge into one because you have been made whole.

I remember the first time I saw him. I was going home to my *Abuela* when I saw this stranger. He was obviously a stranger based on his expensive clothes. We the people of Puebla de Cruz are a simple rural people. He stopped me then asked for the location of the orphanage. I watched his lips as he talked, he clearly didn't know how to pronounce the names around here.

I used my hands and showed him that he should continue down the road where he will meet a fork, then he should take his right, then another right and that is where he would find the orphanage home.

"*Gracias*," he said.

And I nodded. If the angels were to appear to me and tell me that I had just met the love of my life I would never have believed. But if it was Maria de las Mercedes, of course I would believe. I didn't see him again until a week later. I was away from work because my *Abuelo* was sick. I work as the cleaner in the only hotel in our village. My boss, Señor Padilla, is a very nice man and I wondered how he was coping without me.

"I have a temporary cleaner," he informed me when I resumed.

I gave him a quizzical look so he elaborated.

"We have a new guest in the hotel. He could only afford to pay for a night so we came up with an arrangement, or he did. He would clean the place in exchange for his stay in the hotel. He says he came to look for a lost relative."

I wasn't thrilled about this development, but Señor Padilla assured me that it wouldn't affect my job. I went round the rooms to see what kind of work the 'usurper' did and I wasn't impressed. Clearly he hadn't learnt the fine art of finishing. I applied my pristine touch to the rooms then I went to take out the trash but then I discovered that there was only one bag left. The new cleaner must have taken the rest. I carried the bag then walked to the refuse dump and dumped the refuse.

It started to rain suddenly so I began to run back to the hotel but I was drenched before I could reach. Señor Padilla began to laugh at me when I arrived. I laughed too as the situation was humorous but then I stopped when someone touched me from behind. It was the stranger, with an umbrella in his hand.

"I saw you running in the rain. I called you so that you could come under my umbrella. Didn't you hear me?"

"No she can't. She is deaf," said Señor Padilla.

Of course I didn't hear Señor Padilla say those words, but the expression on the face of the stranger is one I know all too well. Señor Padilla introduced us, that was when I got to know his name and that he was the new cleaner.

In case you have been wondering all this while, my name is Mercedes Mendoza. I became deaf at the age of twelve due to a car accident where I lost both parents. And ever since, I have been living with my grandparents. I can read lips and everybody in our small community knows to face me when talking to me, but visitors of course don't, hence the awkward situation we are now in.

"Nice to meet you. My name is Mercedes," I said.

I could still speak but it sounded like I had water in my mouth as people told me.

"Nice to meet you too. My name is Diego."

We waited for the rain to stop then we continued with our work. Day after day I watched him work. I know that he is a wealthy man not because of the watch he wore but by everything else. And yet he didn't act as if cleaning after people was beneath him. He was a man of mystery and humility, which is one reason I fell in love with him. We barely spoke to each other, but I could tell that something was weighing on his shoulders.

Things were good at work but back home my *Abuelo's* condition got worse. He needed medical attention, not the kind the Sisters or the hospital here could give. We needed to take him to town. My *Abuela* and I gathered all the money we had. I went to Señor Padilla to ask for his assistance to drive us to town and he obliged, leaving Diego in charge.

My grandfather was admitted but we couldn't pay for his treatment. We were so distraught and didn't know what to do. I returned home with Señor Padilla to try and raise some money while my grandmother stayed behind. I went to the Sisters and friends of the family but what I could raise in three days was a small fraction of what was needed. Hopefully the hospital would take this while I look for the rest. But shockingly enough, when I got to the hospital, I learnt that an anonymous benefactor had settled the bill and that my *Abuelo* was responding to treatment. Who was this mysterious benefactor? I asked myself. And I got the answer two days after my grandfather returned from the hospital.

I was cleaning Diego's room as it was in the section I was assigned for the day. I was emptying his trash when I discovered the hospital receipt with his and my grandfather's name and the amount he paid. He was our anonymous benefactor but never said a word to me.

I sat down on a chair because I was overwhelmed by his magnanimity. If he had this kind of money why did he… I was asking myself then it dawned on me. For the passed few days I have noticed that he wasn't wearing his watch. Instead of throwing the receipt away, I pocketed it. I waited till closing time to thank him.

"Thank you for paying for my *Abuelo's* hospital bills," I said to him.

He looked at me surprised, and realising that he couldn't deny it he said, "You are welcome. Please don't tell anyone."

I nodded my head but had to invite him over for dinner though I never told my grandparents why. And from then, he began to peel off those thick layers of mystery he shrouded himself with. One night, just as I was about to go home, I saw him talking with Sr. Rebecca. It looked private so I had no intention of inquiring what it was about. But he saw me looking at them, and the next day he told me everything.

"I am looking for my biological mother," he confided in me.

He told me the circumstances of his birth and the events that brought him here including his cheating girlfriend. Sr. Rebecca remembered him and was glad to see him all grown. Unfortunately, she hasn't been able to find any records of his biological parents. His mother disappeared as quickly as she appeared.

"It is painful not knowing where you come from," I said to him. "But you have a family that loves you, a father who cares for you and will be worried about your whereabouts. Call them," I advised. "So that they know you are safe."

He took my advice partly. Señor Padilla had a telephone in the hotel that barely worked, and when it did, had weak signal. So Diego called his trusted friend to let him know where he is and inquired about his family. Maria de la Rosa was fine, but he hadn't seen Diego's father in a while, in fact no one has. Diego guessed that maybe his father too needed time alone.

Diego and I spent more time together and it was inevitable, we fell in love.

"Don't get me wrong," he said to me. "But I am happy that your past relationships failed."

Those words can only be romantic if they are said to you by your soulmate. And we are, soulmates. My grandparents welcomed him with open arms. He came to this village in search of his family, and though not as he had imagined, but he found his family.

He accompanied me to my parents' graves on the Day of the Dead. I told him stories of my parents and he told me stories of his adopted mother as his father told him. It is always a sad day for me but he comforted me.

"It is good that we tell each other these stories," he said to me.

"Why?" I asked.

"So that our children will remember their ancestors."

"Our children?" I asked, which caused his eyes to widen with surprise. He then looked down so I couldn't see what he was saying.

He finally looked up and said, "I think we should leave here."

"Where do you want us to go?"

"Just follow me," he said.

He took me to Rio Alonso which got its name from the founding father of Puebla de Cruz.

Normally by this time of the day the river will be filled with people. But because of the festivities that came with the Day of the Dead, no one was here. It is a romantic spot and I was wondering why Diego brought me here. I turned to ask then I saw him bring out a box from his pocket. He got down on one knee, opened the box and revealed a beautiful ring. He placed it on his lap then he began to sign to me.

He had learnt quite a bit of sign language, and he chooses it to speak to me because sometimes I may misread people's lips. I know proposing with words can be romantic. But when it is done in sign language, it is more romantic because every gesture has more meaning and it truly comes from the heart. I will translate what he said.

"Destiny can take you to places you never knew existed. I came in search of my mother but then I found you Mercedes, *mi amor, mi Corazon*. You are my destiny and it has taken me this long to find you. If only my mother had raised me up here where I was born, I would have met you a long time ago. But fate has brought us together, and I promise that I will never let you go, not now, not ever.

It is with gratitude and humility that on this day, I, Diego Antonio Gutierrez, ask you *mi amor preciosa,*

Mercedes Catalina Mendoza, to be my wife and the mother of our children."

I didn't need to think much or say anything. I nodded my head as tears flowed freely from my eyes. I knelt in front of him and then he put the ring on my finger. We hugged each other and kissed and we made love for the first time.

We kept our engagement secret for three days then we told my grandparents who told our neighbours who told their cousins. Soon everybody, even the monks, knew that the deaf lady is engaged. Señor Padilla was planning on throwing us an engagement party in the hotel. Arrangements were on the way but things changed when he got a phone call.

"Diego," he said. "Someone called Flavio has been calling asking to speak to you. He says it is urgent."

Diego called back and that was when he got the news that his father was terminally ill and wanted to see him.

"I have to go back," he said to me, after informing me of his father's health. "You should come with me, my father will be happy to see his future daughter-in-law."

Everything was quick and unexpected, so I said, "Go ahead without me. I can't leave my grandparents so sudden."

"Okay, I will come back in a week or two to get you. By then you would have arranged all that is necessary."

I gave him the money he needed for his fare back home. He gave me his number to reach him. He left with no luggage but with my heart and dreams. It took him three days to get home. He called and informed Señor Padilla that he had arrived safely. Unfortunately I wasn't there when he called. I tried the next day but his number wasn't going through. I kept on trying but still no response.

Christmas came and went and still there was no word from Diego. I so badly wanted to talk to him. I wanted to tell him that I was pregnant with our child. Then on New Year's Eve, a friend said she saw Diego going to Señor Padilla's hotel. I couldn't contain my joy as I ran to see the love of my life. I ran faster than I had ever ran in my life and was almost out of breath when I came close to the hotel.

I saw him and another man get into a car. I tried to shout but I had no voice, and whatever sound I made could be mistaken for a bird. I watched as the car began to move. I was about ten feet away from my love but he didn't see me. I chased after the vehicle, screamed and waved as hard as I could. But Diego drove away without saying a word to me and without learning that he would soon become a father.

I fell on the road and cried bitterly. Why has *mi amor* abandoned us? I picked myself up and went back to the hotel where Señor Padilla was perplexed to learn that Diego had gone without seeing me.

"He came to take his belongings," Señor Padilla said, but that didn't answer all my questions.

At this time my grandparents knew that I was pregnant and wanted Diego to come and marry me and live up to his responsibilities. I had to find him. He told me where he lived but I have never left this village before and for someone like me, it will be difficult to communicate with people. Luckily, Sr. Rebecca was to visit her Sisters of another congregation in the state where Diego lived so she said that I could come with her, but that would be in two weeks time.

When the day came, I got my affairs in order and bade farewell to my *Abuelo* and *Abuela*. It was indeed a tedious journey, but we got help along the way as they saw Sr. Rebecca in her habit. We slept in the convent when we arrived and two days later we went in search of Diego. Apparently, *Hacienda de Gutierrez* wasn't that hard to locate. The gate was wide open when we arrived, there was a *fiesta* of some kind. Diego will be happy to see me and will be most excited to hear the news.

"We are looking for Diego Gutierrez," Sr. Rebecca said to one of the men decorating the place.

He made some gestures then Sr. Rebecca asked me to follow her. We came to a place where there was a beehive of activities. We were just about to make further inquiry when Sr. Rebecca turned me to herself and said.

"I think I just saw someone that I believed was dead. Please wait here while I go and confirm that my eyes were not deceiving me."

I nodded, then she left. And there I waited until I too saw someone familiar. It looked like him but his gait was different, pompous. So I went to clear my doubt and as I walked closer I realised that it was indeed my Diego. I ran to him, held him on his right arm, turned him towards me and hugged him. I was so happy to be reunited with him and cried tears of joy. Those few seconds felt like heaven before he pushed me away.

"Yes," he said. "How do we know each other?"

Those words almost took the breath out of me but it was nothing compared to the way he looked at me, indifferent, like I was a stranger. I wanted to speak, he said he loved the sound of my unique watery voice but my heart was too heavy to let my lips move. So I signed;

'Why are you doing this? Why do you act as if you don't know who I am?'

He still had that look on his face.

"Sorry I don't understand sign language. Are you one of my relatives? If you are, welcome to my wedding, it is so good to have you here."

If there were any words that could kill the soul, those were it. This is his wedding, that is why he is pretending not to know me. He had been lying to me all this while, he had been pretending. I thought he loved me but it was all a lie, a lie which has led to the baby in my womb.

I was heartbroken to say the least. I had to cut all ties with him. I tried to remove his engagement ring, but no matter what I did it wouldn't come off. He stood there just looking at me. I couldn't bear the heartache and the disgrace anymore so I decided to leave. I found Sr. Rebecca in the spot where she asked me to wait for her. She had a look of surprise on her face but it soon changed to concern when she saw me.

"Did you find Diego?"

"Please let's leave here immediately," I pleaded, so we did.

I didn't say a word throughout the journey. It was thirty minutes after we got back to the convent that I told her everything. She was shocked but not as shocked as I was when she told me who she saw.

"I saw Diego's biological mother."

"At the wedding?"

"Yes."

"This is incredible. Does she know that he is her son? Does he know that his long lost mother is at his wedding?"

"She had no idea that Diego is her son. And I sense that she would not tell him."

"He has to know," I said, as I stood up. He hurt me deeply, but if I could make his search end then I would. "I have to tell him. What does she look like?"

"She is wearing a red dress. It will be difficult not to pick her out from the crowd."

I cleaned my face, put on my shoes and went back to *Hacienda de Gutierrez*. It was less busy now.

"Please where can I find Diego?" I asked one of the help.

"They are over there," he said, as he pointed up a hill.

There was a road that led up but following it would take me longer because it was meant for vehicles. As the village girl that I am, I chose instead to follow the quicker footpath up the hill. I made it to the top but then I couldn't move further because I saw Diego and he saw me, and in his eyes I saw the man that loved me. But it seems my good intentions were the death of me, because I arrived just as he was making his vows.

In tears my friend Diego continued his tale. He arrived home and found his dying father on his bed. Jorge Gutierrez had been suffering from cancer but no one knew. Now here he was, in his final days. And all he wanted was to have his family by his side.

"*Familia es todo*," he said to Diego.

"Si *Padre*," replied Diego.

He didn't bore him with the details of where he went. These moments were precious and he wanted to make them as pleasant as possible. He spent the night by his father's side. Early the next morning, Rosita called him and said;

"Diego, here is a list of drugs. Please go to the pharmacy and get them."

"Right away."

He got into his car and drove off. The road was clear except for a vehicle which came up next to him. Thinking that the car was going to overtake him, Diego didn't mind. But instead it came closer to him. Diego turned and looked at the car. He was shocked to see that it was Alba and her lover. If this was an apology, it was strange and unwanted. So he decided to speed up. But before he could speed up, Alba brought out a gun and shot at him. She missed but this caused him to lose control of the car and he drove off a bridge. His car fell head-on thirty feet to the bottom of a shallow river. And that was all he remembered, or maybe not.

He woke up hours later in the hospital with the doctor by his side and Alba at his feet with her right hand in her purse.

"Where am I?" he asked. "What happened?"

"You are in a hospital Señor Gutierrez," answered the doctor. "You were in an accident. Luckily some squalid gold miners heard the crash and rescued you. Can you look at me?" He flashed his light on Diego's eyes. "Do you remember what date it is?"

"Date? I honestly don't keep dates in my head."

"Okay then. Do you know who she is?"

"Yes," answered Diego. "That is Alba *mi Chula del fuego.*"

This was the point I and my wife entered the room. I noticed that Alba looked surprised and I remember her taking her hand from her purse and zipping it.

"Is that right?" the doctor asked Alba smiling. "Are you his *Chula del fuego*?"

"Yes I am. I am his fiancée," answered Alba.

"Fiancée?" asked a surprised Diego.

"Yes we are engaged, don't you remember?"

We all looked at Diego, something was wrong and it was confirmed by his next statement.

"The only people engaged here are Flavio and Maria de la Rosa."

"Diego," said Maria de la Rosa. "We are not engaged. Flavio and I are married, for like a year now."

"What's the last thing you remember?" the doctor asked.

"I remember your engagement party and… that is the last thing I remember."

"Diego that was like two years ago," I said.

It was now clear, Diego was suffering from amnesia. Almost two years of his life had been wiped clean.

He remained silent for a minute or two before he spoke again.

"So we are engaged?"

"Yes," Alba said.

"But why don't we know about it?" asked Maria de la Rosa.

"It is true," I said. "Before Diego left town he told me that he was going to propose to her. I guess he did."

"Yes, exactly," said Alba, though she didn't have any ring to prove it. "Will his memories come back?"

"It may or may not," answered the doctor. "It is hard to tell. We will keep him under observation and I will ask you not to overwhelm him with memorabilia but just a little to help jog his memory."

Diego stayed in the hospital for five days. It was when he came back home that he experienced the pain of hearing about his father's health for the second time.

"I know this is a tough time for you Diego," his father said. "But there is one thing that I will ask of you. I don't know how many days or hours I have left. So I will like to see you get married before I die."

"Of course father, anything you ask of me."

And so, we began to prepare for his wedding. Diego looked happy on the outside, but because I know him so well, I knew that deep down he wasn't happy. Something in him was missing. He looked like the same Diego, walked like the same Diego, talked like the same Diego. But this was not the true Diego. His sense of self, his ego was missing.

I was the only one he told about his trip, so I began to fill in the blanks little by little. He never told me about Mercedes until the day of his wedding. If he had, we wouldn't be in this quagmire that we are in now.

"I have to go there," he said. "Maybe I kept some documents in my hotel room."

"I will come with you."

We informed everyone about our trip - his last days as a bachelor, we called it.

"I know you Diego, but don't bring any lady close to my husband."

"I won't Maria de la Rosa."

"When will you be back?" she asked.

"Mañana," I answered, which calmed her down.

We took the private jet. Jorge Gutierrez also bought six cargo planes to expand his business and Diego being his successor, would be in charge of everything. We rented a car after we landed. It was a terrible journey to Puebla de Cruz, the roads were in bad condition. We located the hotel and were greeted by the owner as soon as we entered.

"Welcome back Diego," said Señor Padilla.

"Thank you," Diego said, pretending like he remembered the man.

"How are preparations for your wedding?"

"Oh, we are going about it just fine."

It seems news of Diego's wedding has spread to this part of the country, I thought to myself.

"May I have the keys to my old room? I think I forgot something."

"Oh Diego, why do you act like a stranger? Here," Señor Padilla hands him the key with the room number on the key holder. "You and your friend are free to spend as long as you want."

Diego collects the key and did his best to disguise what he was feeling, which is, how can he spend a night in this wretched hotel. We went to the room and searched but unfortunately we found nothing.

"The last time we spoke you told me that no one knew your mother. But it is good that we came. Does anything look or feel familiar?"

"*Nada*. We should leave. There is no point wasting time looking for a mother who abandoned me when my father only has days to live."

We bade farewell to the hotelier.

"I will drive us back," Diego said, then I handed him the key.

He drove with his eyes forward to the future. He left his past behind and didn't care to look at the rear-view mirror. We got back home and continued from where we left off. The wedding is to take place in their estate because of Jorge's health. He looked brighter and happier, and on the day of the wedding, he looked healthy like he wasn't sick. Diego and Mateo helped him get dressed and together with Maria de la Rosa they spent a long time with him because they didn't know how much time they had left with him.

It was inevitable that Diego would have to leave them to prepare for his wedding. So he did, and that was when he met Mercedes. Everything was confusing at first, but as he walked to his room, he began to remember, he began to remember what Alba did to him, which was painful, but not as painful as when he remembered his beautiful Mercedes. His heart broke as he realised the pain he caused her by not remembering her and treating her like a stranger. His ring was still on her finger which meant that what they had can still be salvaged.

"I have to find her," he says to me.

"Where? Where do you think she went?"

"I don't know but I must find her."

So we went round the house and asked if anyone had seen her but unfortunately no one has. We decided to drive out and when we came to the gate, we asked the security there.

"Yes, we saw her when she left," says one of the men. "Señora Rosita left not long after."

"*Gracias*," we both say, then Diego zoomed off.

We searched every bus stop and asked around but no one saw or knew her. So we decided to try the less travelled roads. It is less than an hour to his wedding and he intends on finding and explaining to her then bring her back home and they would get married.

Thick bushes were on both sides of this lonely road. It was hopeless, until we spotted Rosita's car almost completely hidden in one of the bushes.

"We should ask her if she saw Mercedes on her way out," says Diego, which was not the first thought that came to my mind to ask her.

We treaded carefully into the bush and soon afterwards we heard Rosita's voice in an argument. We crept closer until we had a clear view but we made sure that we were hidden by the bushes. Rosita was surrounded by seven men and one of them was Alba's lover.

"*Jefe*," he says, as he points a gun at Rosita. "You should have killed her."

The boss motioned him to bring down the gun. He stepped forward and smacked Rosita on the face which caused her to fall. Diego wanted to come out of the bush but I held him back. The boss takes off his dark shades and then we see his face clearly. He is Sergio Fernandez the head of *El Cartel de las Tres Calaveras* (The Three Skulls Cartel).

"Thirty four years ago you and your boyfriend stole my money and ran away. We caught and killed him but you and the money were nowhere to be found. Stand up, stand up Raquel." He helps Rosita to her feet. "You are unworthy of that name, Innocent."

"I will pay you back your money. I will help smuggle your drugs on his cargo planes. Please don't kill Diego."

"Why the sudden change of heart Raquel?" asked Sergio. "You were the one who came up with this plan after Alba discovered who you were. I wanted to kill you but you pleaded and said you could use your husband's ships and planes to smuggle drugs for us then I reconsidered but Alba must be employed in the company to watch over you. But when you discovered that she and Diego were dating you realised that we will no longer need you. And being an ambitious woman you said…"

"I said that even if Diego and Alba are married that she wouldn't have complete access. So kill him after the wedding and my son who does everything I say will become the head of the company and you will have unlimited access."

"You are a very resourceful woman Raquel, a survivor. But now, you come to me with a change of heart and beg me to spare his life and that you will pay back what you stole. For a woman you have a lot of *cojones*. What caused you to change your mind?"

Rosita remained silent.

"Answer me!" he says as he slaps her.

She falls to the ground.

"Oh, you are bleeding," says Sergio. "Well it doesn't matter. No one will notice the bloodstain on your red dress."

"I think we should leave now Diego before they come this way," I say to my friend.

"I want more than what you and your dead boyfriend stole from me. I want to expand my empire especially now that the rival Five Daggers Cartel is no more. And you Raquel, will see to this. The plan will continue as planned and if you try to stop it, then I will kill you."

It was clear that they were about to leave so Diego and I ran away as fast and as stealthy as we could. There are hundreds of questions in my mind but I had to wait for us to get to the car and have driven far away before I could ask.

"What are you going to do now?" I ask, but Diego was completely silent.

We arrive back at the family estate a few minutes to the wedding.

"Where have you been Diego?" Mateo asks. "Everyone is waiting for you. Father is already there. I couldn't ruin his happiness when he asked why you aren't there yet."

"Father," Diego says, the only word he has spoken since we left the bush. "I will be out soon, tell everyone that the wedding will soon commence."

Mateo leaves the room and Diego closes the door behind him.

"You were joking when you told him that the wedding will continue as planned, right?"

"No I wasn't," says Diego, but I didn't think I heard him right.

"Tell me that you are joking."

"No I am not. What will happen if I told everyone what we just saw? Our home will be destroyed. My father's days are numbered and I want to make him happy for the remainder of it. *Familia es todo* he said to me. I am the head of the family now and I have to think about everyone's safety."

"What about your safety?"

"That comes last," he answered quickly.

"I can understand you doing this for your father. But I think he will be happier living his last days knowing that his children are not in danger because of that evil Rosita. Call off the wedding Diego, call off the wedding."

"If I do they will kill my stepmother."

"Don't tell me this is because of her."

Diego looks at me. He takes a deep breath in then out and says;

"I know you will not understand, but there is something in me that tells me to protect her. I feel this connection to her that I can not explain nor do I care to have it explained. All that I know is that I must protect her at all cost."

With his mind made up, we made our way up the hill. Rosita was there already. I saw her staring at Diego with tears in her eyes. I honestly don't know if they were crocodile tears, tears of sadness or tears of joy. Not long after we got to the altar, Alba *la bruja* processed in. I wanted to say something but he made me promise not to say anything.

"Do you, Diego Antonio Gutierrez take…"

I can't believe that Diego is about to make this vow to Alba before God and his family. But he says;

"I do."

He had tears in his eyes as he said this. He wasn't looking at his bride, his gaze was afar. I followed it and then saw what or who he cwas looking at. There is no doubt in my mind that she was Mercedes. He did what he did for his family and for Rosita for some reason. But now I know he wonders, AM I A FOOL?

PART 6

Judge George

Characters

JUDGE GEORGE - Radio presenter

VICTOR ANDREWS - Gender activist and guest of radio program

AMINA SALISU - Gender activist and guest of radio program

CALLER 1 - A woman

CALLER 1's FIANCE

CALLER 2 - A woman

CALLER 3 - A woman

CALLER 4 - A man

THREE WORKERS

CHILD 1 - Child of Judge George

THE WIFE - Wife of Judge George

2 SLEEPING CHILDREN

ACT I

A RADIO STATION. Three people are seated with a table between them. A man and a woman on the left side of the table while another man is on the right. They have mics in front of them and above them on the wall is the ON AIR sign which is turned on. A speaker phone is at the centre of the table.

Around the room are posters of the radio station KNW 102.5 and that of the program JUDGE GEORGE with the face of the man on the right on it.

Three other people are seen walking around silently fixing the mics and other things.

[The Theme song plays]

JUDGE GEORGE: It is 2:30pm on a beautiful Tuesday afternoon. I woke up this morning feeling refreshed and excited because of the discussion we will be having today. If you are just joining us, you are just in time. This is your favourite talk-show on radio, Judge George, on your favourite station KNW 102.5. And I am your host Judge George, here to pronounce judgement on any dispute you bring to me, be it on the streets or in your homes. This show is known for its objectivity and unbiased nature. So feel free to call and I will give my judgement, isn't it?

VICTOR ANDREWS: Yes, it is.

AMINA SALISU: It definitely is.

JUDGE GEORGE: Before I tell you our topic for discussion today, I will like to introduce my guests. I will first of all start with the lady, as the saying goes - ladies first. She is by name Mrs. Amina Salisu, and she is the country admin and logistics manager of Hope; an NGO that fights against gender inequality.

AMINA SALISU: Thank you for having me on your program. I am delighted to be here. I never miss your program. Every Tuesday by 2:30pm I am glued to my radio.

JUDGE GEORGE: Thank you, and I am honoured to have you here with us. My second guest is Mr. Victor Andrews. He is the state coordinator for a non-profit organisation called Together We Stand, which fights for gender equality.

VICTOR ANDREWS: Yes. Thank you Judge George. It is a pleasure being here. I too am an avid listener of your program.

JUDGE GEORGE: You are welcome Mr. Andrews. I don't think I need to say much, I believe the topic for discussion is already clear. We will be discussing on gender equality or gender inequality depending on who you ask. My guests are on the same mission but… [the phone blinks] Oh, we already have a caller. Well let's see what he or she has to say. [He picks the call] Hello and welcome to the program. How may I be the judge in your case today?

CALLER 1 [a woman]: Good afternoon Judge George. I am having a serious problem with my fiancé.

JUDGE GEORGE: Yes go on.

CALLER 1: Our traditional wedding is coming up and he insists that I must kneel down when I present him with wine. I told him that I will never kneel down to any man. This is an archaic tradition that subjugates women. I might call off the wedding if he insists.

JUDGE GEORGE: Is your fiancé there with you?

CALLER 1'S FIANCE: Yes I am.

JUDGE GEORGE: That's good, because if I am to judge this case both parties must be there. Your case is apt for our topic today. Before I make my judgement, I will like to ask a question. How did he propose to you?

CALLER 1: Well, my parents asked me to come home for a family meeting. I thought it was something serious so I rushed back home only to discover that it was a surprise. He came in front of me and knelt down on one knee and asked me to be his wife and I…

JUDGE GEORGE: That is all I needed to hear. You said he knelt down before you in front of your family and friends to propose to you, isn't it?

CALLLER 1: Yes.

JUDGE GEORGE: Then why can't you do the same?

[Caller 1's fiancé laughs in the background]

CALLER 1: Because it is not the same.

JUDGE GEORGE: How is it not the same thing? He knelt before you. Why can't you reciprocate?

CALLER 1: Because it is what men do. They kneel to propose, it is romantic.

JUDGE GEORGE: Okay, let me ask another question. Who is older between the two of you?

CALLER 1: He is.

JUDGE GEORGE: I believe you both come from a culture where it is a taboo for an elder to kneel for someone younger. But he did that for you. MY JUDGEMENT [theme song plays]. You have to kneel for your husband on your wedding day. [Theme song ends] Now back to our guests. Where was I?

AMINA SALISU: You were talking about our missions.

JUDGE GEORGE: Yes. My two guests are on the same mission of gender equality but are advocating somewhat different paths to get there. I will ask Mr. Andrews to speak further on how he wants to achieve this.

VICTOR ANDREWS: Thank you Judge George. I like your judgement on the first case today. When a woman kneels before a man it is gender discrimination, but when a man kneels before a woman it is romantic. That is the idea I want to change when we talk about gender inequality. Some rules have to be changed, but we must maintain the balance.

AMINA SALISU: And what is the balance?

VICTOR ANDREWS: Women must remain women and men must remain men. Gender equality is about making sure that both genders are respected for who they are.

JUDGE GEORGE: So what are your thoughts on this Mrs. Salisu?

AMINA SALISU: Thank you Judge George. First of all it is not the same thing. When a man kneels before a woman, it is with one knee. But when a woman kneels before a man it is with both knees to the ground like a servant, hence, the discrimination.

JUDGE GEORGE: That is because men wear trousers and women wear skirts. Even if she wears a trouser, once her legs are parted like that it could send the wrong message.

VICTOR ANDREWS: Exactly. To add to my previous point; a woman's need for romance is the equivalent of a man's need for respect. He kneels and proposes, he opens the door for her even though she is capable of doing it herself. She kneels to present their wedding wine, she brings his food from the kitchen and serves him even though he is capable of doing it himself. There should be a balance and everyone should be given what makes them feel appreciated.

AMINA SALISU: When a man doesn't do what you said, no one would tell him that it is wrong. But when a woman doesn't, society will hound on her for not doing that.

VICTOR ANDREWS: There is a bias I agree one hundred percent. But we only tend to look at one aspect; that against women. If you can list a billion biases against women, you can also get a billion biases against men, equivalent to those suffered by women.

JUDGE GEORGE: We have a second caller [he picks the call]. Hello and welcome to the program. How may I be the judge in your case today?

CALLER 2 [a woman]: Good afternoon Judge George, it is me Rose your number one caller.

JUDGE GEORGE: But today you called in second [he laughs], just kidding. What case do you want me to judge for you today?

CALLER 2: I like your judgement on my case last week. For that reason I am calling so that you can tell some people; I will not mention names, that times have changed.

VICTOR ANDREWS: Times have changed really.

CALLER 2: I attend my friends' churches when they invite me and women are not asked or forced to cover our hair. But when I go back to my church, they insist that all women must cover their hair. I have had this question for a long time but because of the topic today, I decided to bring it up. Please let them know that it is discriminatory against women to be forced to cover their hair when men don't, thank you.

JUDGE GEORGE: Rose, Rose, she is back again. Now, if I must tackle this matter, I must go at it practically. Time will change, sometimes for the better and sometimes for the worse. But we must never lose our essence. If you are going by 1 Corinthians chapter 11, I can understand your anger. But that is how the law was interpreted for people of those days. Times will change but the essence of God's laws remains. Let's look at it practically, we live in a man's world and have more kings than queens right?

VICTOR ANDREWS: Yes.

AMINA SALISU: Unfortunately.

JUDGE GEORGE: If the king is a Christian, whenever he comes to church or is invited to another church, because men take off their caps in church, he would have to take off his symbol of authority, his crown, or leave it at home to show that God is king. Even if he is alone and he wants to pray, he will take off his cap to show that God is king. As for women, you all know, your hair is your crown.

AMINA SALISU: Yes it is, but my people are conservative and we don't show it much. But as you said, times are changing and we are changing too.

JUDGE GEORGE: A woman's hair is her crown of glory. You spend a lot of time and money on your hair. But can you, for the sake of God, cover that which is so dear to you to show that God is your crown? Can you cover your hair in private when you are praying because you want to show that God is your crown? If you do that, that humility will show in everything you do. MY JUDGEMENT [theme song plays]. If you are asked to cover your hair it is not wrong. [Theme song ends]

VICTOR ANDREWS: You get my point. Men not covering their hair and women covering their hair in church is not gender inequality, but gender equality.

JUDGE GEORGE: So what you are saying is that; Men are men, women are women, the same rules don't apply, but treat them both as human beings.

VICTOR ANDREWS: Exactly.

JUDGE GEORGE: We were talking about biases suffered by women and men before the second call came. Mrs. Amina, I will like you to elucidate on this.

AMINA SALISU: Since the beginning of time, even before recorded history, women have been subjugated and treated as third class citizens. Even their sons whom they bore and raised will one day exercise authority over their mothers because they are men.

When we speak we are not heard. Whatever we have achieved is not celebrated; history doesn't remember women. We live in the same world but we were denied the right to exercise our franchise. We had to fight for women's suffrage. It was not until 1995 in the Beijing women conference that the world began to listen to us.

JUDGE GEORGE: And it is a good thing that we have started to pay more attention to our women. Mr. Victor, what can you add to this?

VICTOR ANDREWS: I agree with her. History doesn't remember women. Maybe because it is spelt as His Story not Her Story or Their…

JUDGE GEORGE: Sorry, we have another caller. [He picks the call] Hello and welcome to the program. How may I be the judge in your case today?

CALLER 3 [a woman]: Good afternoon, my name is Karen. I am on the phone with my friend Agatha. We would like you to judge our case and bring an end to our debate.

JUDGE GEORGE: Yes go on. What is the debate all about?

CALLER 3: Men are scum. I am honestly tired of dating. My friend Agatha says I should not give up on love and that all men are not the same but I disagree. All men are the same and men are scum. Please judge our case, thank you.

JUDGE GEORGE: The answer to this is simple but you have to consider every part. MY JUDGEMENT [theme song plays]. Are all men the same? Yes. But! There will always be exceptions to the rule be it positive or negative [Theme song ends]. And please men are not scum, if we are, that includes your father, brothers, sons, nephews and so on.
Now back to you Mr. Victor.

VICTOR ANDREWS: Yes, history doesn't remember women or their achievements. But there is a side to that that some women benefit from.

AMINA SALISU: How do you mean?

VICTOR ANDREWS: It is in recorded history that men have committed many atrocities against humanity. But women have also done that and because history doesn't remember them, those acts are forgotten.

JUDGE GEORGE: That is an interesting way of looking at history.

VICTOR ANDREWS: We must go about achieving gender equality with full transparency and honesty. Women have borne the brunt most of the time but that doesn't mean that they are always innocent. Like I said before, If you can list a billion biases against women, you can also get a billion biases against men. The only difference is that men don't talk about it because they are men.

AMINA SALISU: I will like to know the kind of bias men suffer.

VICTOR ANDREWS: When a couple gets divorced, the woman is automatically given full or primary custody. What about the father? Men have to fight for custody of their own children. And after custody has been settled, the man still gets fewer days to spend with his children.

AMINA SALISU: Okay, go on.

VICTOR ANDREWS: Right from a very tender age, life is harder for boys than girls. It is just that they are taught not to talk but carry their responsibilities as men. A boy and a girl will come late to school. The girl will be given a menial punishment while the boy will be whipped or given a more severe punishment. He doesn't complain because it is part of his being to protect a woman.
Even in the bible, Sarah doubted and laughed when an angel told her that she would have a son. But the God of the Old Testament who answers by fire, says her son will be called Isaac because she laughed. But when the same offence was committed by Zachariah in the New Testament, God made him dumb until his son was born.

AMINA SALISU: So you are saying that God is gender-biased?

VICTOR ANDREWS: What I am saying is that there is a lot of responsibility on a man's head, which therefore means more judgement and punishment should he fail.

AMINA SALISU: Then you should communicate to us more and let us help.

VICTOR ANDREWS: That will help but don't seek to become men in the process.

AMINA SALISU: How do you mean?

JUDGE GEORGE: I think what he means is that; Men are men, women are women, the same rules don't apply, but treat them both as human beings.

VICTOR ANDREWS: Exactly. There is this film I watched called Hidden Figures. There was a scene where the middle daughter was angry that the first child got a bed all to herself while she had to share a bed with her younger sister. Her mother told her that the first child gets a bed to herself because of the responsibilities she has. But if she the middle child wants a bed all to herself, then she would have to do the chores of the elder one. After considering this, the middle child changed her mind.

JUDGE GEORGE: I think I know where you are going with this.

VICTOR ANDREWS: The world is arranged that way. Women may try, but it is ultimately the responsibility of a man to take care of everyone and everything. And because of that, he gets some privileges in the society that women don't.

AMINA SALISU: You are not putting into account that women have become the breadwinner and sole provider in some families. But still when she speaks no one hears her because she is not a man. She puts in the work but doesn't get her deserved promotion so that she can take care of her family because she is not a man. She works thrice as hard and shouts before anyone hears her.

VICTOR ANDREWS: You are right, which is why I am advocating for equal work equal pay. I will get to that point later. What I am trying to say is that men get privileges in society that women don't because they are men. Women get privileges in society that men don't because they are women.

JUDGE GEORGE: Can you elaborate more on that?

VICTOR ANDREWS: Certainly. A woman can live the whole of her life knowing that she will never be asked to pick up arms to protect her country or be conscripted into the army in times of war. If the men are few, little boys are turned into child-soldiers even when there are adult girls and women around. During war, women and children are protected though some soldiers don't abide by this rule. But because a man is a man, he has to sacrifice his life to protect his family.

Women fight for inclusiveness in everything but when they say they should stay at home with the children during war time they won't claim gender bias.

AMINA SALISU: I don't know what it is you are talking about. Women go into battle. Haven't you seen female soldiers in Afghanistan?

VICTOR ANDREWS: Yes they are there because they are soldiers, but also because they are women. Afghanistan is a conservative society and the male soldiers can't talk to or even come close to an Afghan woman. So women soldiers are brought in.

JUDGE GEORGE: So their work is gender based.

VICTOR ANDREWS: Yes. I wouldn't advice that they seek to be more in the field like their male counterparts because of gender equality. As long as men are men, if a woman is with him on the battleground, his mind will not be settled. Somewhere at the back of his mind he will be worried and want to protect her or he may be aroused and distracted.

AMINA SALISU: Women are always the damsels in distress. We always need saving.

JUDGE GEORGE: I think I should come in here. I
understand why you are angry because women are
always portrayed as being weak and need men to
save them. Writers of the past created this
perception.
Ninety percent of the time you can see it the way
you want to see it. But ten percent of the time, see it
from where it truly comes from.

AMINA SALISU: And where is that?

JUDGE GEORGE: Men want to be the ultimate providers for
their families and especially their women. So in his
fiction is where he lives this fantasy. It is not that he
wants her to get into trouble. He just wants to be the
ultimate provider and protector of his family no
matter the situation.

VICTOR ANDREWS: Is that your judgement? [He laughs]

JUDGE GEORGE: Yes, that's my final judgement. [The
theme song plays then comes to an end] Now Mrs.
Amina what would you like to say?

AMINA SALISU: Actually nothing. During conversations
men don't usually speak, but my colleague here is
speaking for the first time. I will like to hear what
he has to say.

JUDGE GEORGE: Well Mr. Victor, the floor is yours.

VICTOR ANDREWS: Thank you. Men are celebrated more than women, but mothers are celebrated more than fathers.

AMINA SALISU: So a woman must be married or have legitimate children to be celebrated?

VICTOR ANDREWS: Unfortunately that is the world we live in and that perception has to change.

JUDGE GEORGE: I agree.

VICTOR ANDREWS: But that is one of the things women enjoy in society that men don't. Just this year alone I have celebrated about three Mother's Day. I honestly don't know when Father's Day is.

AMINA SALISU: Everyday is Father's Day or Men's Day. We only get few days in a year.

JUDGE GEORGE: Okay.

VICTOR ANDREWS: I just want you to understand the high level of bias that men experience. Fathers are only celebrated after they die. That is when the children, both the sons and daughters, will realise that Daddy really tried.
Gifts are bought for mothers and fathers are neglected. He works hard to provide for everyone and all that he asks for is that he is given his respect. Unmarried men in their twenties and thirties are getting grey and bald. Tell me what will

happen when they become fathers. Fatherhood is a difficult and lonely world. And men being men, they carry their responsibilities in silence.
Motherhood too is extremely difficult. So children honour your fathers and mothers.

AMINA SALISU: I thought maybe you forgot that point.

VICTOR ANDREWS: No I didn't. There is one point I will like to add, and it is the most important of all. Like I said earlier, there are privileges women enjoy in society that men don't because they are women. And there are privileges men enjoy in the society that women don't because they are men.
If I ask you, who dies earlier? Whose life is shorter? Men or women?

AMINA SALISU: Men

JUDGE GEORGE: Men.

VICTOR ANDREWS: Thank you, and because of this, some things in the society are a given for men. They have to work hard to get enough money to marry and take care of their families. They still have to leave behind something for their children after they die. So tell me, how can a man achieve this if he doesn't get such privileges? He speaks and they listen to him. He puts in the work and he has a certain level of guaranty that he will be promoted when the time comes.

Men unfortunately die quicker than women because of the kind of stress and hardship they go through. There are other biological elements that make women live longer. But if women go about gender equality in the wrong way and want to become men. Unfortunately, they will begin to bear the cost that comes with the privileges and die earlier than normal.

I will not be shocked to find out that the death rate in women has increased over the years. That there are more cases of heart attacks and strokes suffered by women. We have different strengths and vulnerabilities. We need to come together to harness our strengths and manage our vulnerabilities.

JUDGE GEORGE: We have a caller on the line. [He picks the call] Hello and welcome to the program. How may I be the judge in your case today?

CALLER 4 [a man]: Hello, my name is Carlos. I will like to commend you for your show. You are doing something amazing and I will like to encourage you to continue.

JUDGE GEORGE: Thank you.

CALLER 4: I don't have a case to be judged. I call instead to add to the topic of discussion today, which is gender inequality. [He pauses] Women are going through hell. Some of them are being abused by their husbands and boyfriends. It is evil and pathetic, and it needs to stop. No man should raise his hands against any woman just because he is physically stronger.

Thank you, that is all I have to say.

JUDGE GEORGE: Straight to the point.

AMINA SALISU: I am happy to hear a man speak about this. Women have carried this burden in silence. I really don't understand why some men do this. If a woman can change her surname to yours, take care of you, why on earth would you abuse her?

JUDGE GEORGE: Absolutely. MY JUDGEMENT [theme song plays]. No man should hit his wife or any woman. [Theme song ends] Mr. Victor, what do you have to add to this?

VICTOR ANDREWS: I completely agree with the caller and the both of you. It is not only physical abuse, but verbal, emotional and mental abuse. I am sure that you have seen a woman who became unrecognisable after marriage. And I am sure that you have seen men whose lives were destroyed by the wives they married.

AMINA SALISU: There are cases where it is the men who are abused by their wives, though they are few. And these men are embarrassed to report these cases.

JUDGE GEORGE: It happens as you said. I have had cases like that on this program. The men remain anonymous of course. It is something we need to talk about more and bring an end to.

AMINA SALISU: Mr. Victor, you always have a different perspective of approaching these topics. What do you have to say now?

JUDGE GEORGE: Yes, give us a broader view like you do.

VICTOR ANDREWS: Thank you. As we address gender violence, it is paramount that we look at it from both sides.

AMINA SALISU: Men are abused too. We know that.

VICTOR ANDREWS: That is not what I am talking about. Men abuse women, and most of the time it is done behind closed doors. When women abuse or assault men, they do it audaciously and in view of everyone. A man may jump the line and a woman may ask him to go back but he would refuse. One thing leads to another and she slaps him, in broad daylight in front of people. As a man he wouldn't fight back. And everyone there would say that he is wrong.
Now imagine a scenario where the genders are reversed. The man will immediately be arrested for assaulting a woman. But in the case of a woman, she would go scot-free after striking a man.

JUDGE GEORGE: Women do that a lot. They can slap a man and say 'do you know me?' 'Do you know who I am?' No one would indict her, and the man who was slapped would just walk away.

VICTOR ANDREWS: We are not saying that spousal abuse is right, but as we tackle it we must tackle it the right way. Couples who are dating or are married. If a man hits the woman once, what should she do? I ask you Mrs. Amina.

AMINA SALISU: It is simple, she should leave that relationship or marriage. If he hits you once he will hit you again.

JUDGE GEORGE: I agree.

VICTOR ANDREWS: I agree with you, but also bear in mind that women are guilty of this too. A couple could be arguing and the man says something hurtful which causes the woman to slap him in expression of her anger. What would you tell the man to do Mrs Amina?

JUDGE GEORGE: It seems like you are attacking her.

VICTOR ANDREWS: I just want us to see things from both sides.

AMINA SALISU: It happens. It happens a lot actually. I will advice him to quit the relationship or the marriage. What he said was wrong but she could have found other ways of expressing her anger.

VICTOR ANDREWS: Good, if she hits you once she will hit you again. But what happens? The man would leave and return later and apologise to the wife for what he said, most of the time. But in some cases he would hit her back, and once that becomes the norm of their relationship, it would be hard to stop.
There are other scenarios where she might not hit him, but throw stuffs at him and damage appliances in the house because she is angry. We don't see that as spousal abuse.

JUDGE GEORGE: As you said, women get away with many things in society.

VICTOR ANDREWS: Yes. And if we want to achieve gender equality, we have to do it right. Women empowerment is a good term because women don't get the chances they deserve. They should be empowered, not to become men, but to have their full rights as human beings. Equity is a term I would prefer than equality. Equality for example means that orange and lemon are the same thing, but they are not. Equity means that orange and lemon are both citrus fruits and should be accorded their respect as such.

AMINA SALISU: You have an interesting way of looking at the world.

VICTOR ANDREWS: [Laughs] Yes I do. Men are men, women are women, the same rules don't apply, but treat them both as human beings.

JUDGE GEORGE: How I wish we had more time to discuss this but unfortunately we have come to the end of today's program. I will ask my guests to make their final statements. To be fair, I will start with the man.

VICTOR ANDREWS: In conclusion, Men are men, women are women, the same rules don't apply, but treat them both as human beings. If you want the best from women, don't treat them or ask them to become men, and vice versa.
Stop the discrimination. An engineer is an engineer, be it a man or a woman. A doctor is a doctor, be it a man or woman. But a woman is an actress while a man is an actor because 99.9% of the roles are gender based. But if women want to call themselves actors, it is still fine.
I am not saying this to ruffle any feathers, but if we want the best in our society, gender roles must be there. Our biological makeups are different. We have our strengths and weaknesses. Men are rough and hard. We can go places and do things women won't find easy to do, and vice versa. It would be difficult for a woman to function in a man's world and vice versa.
Again I will reiterate that I am not trying to hurt anyone. In politics men should have a reasonable majority. And in the military, men should have absolute majority. In sports there should be men and women teams. We should not seek to have a national football team consisting of both men and

women because of gender equality. In that case only transgender men would qualify.

A woman can be a coach of the male team. She might not be able to enter their locker room but being a good coach is not gender based. Women should contest for any political office.

It is a long road ahead of us. But if we must achieve gender equality then men must be involved. Every man comes from a woman. If a woman wants to succeed, a man must be involved. You are a self-made woman, no doubt, you don't need a man. But somewhere along the road there was a man who was pivotal to your success.

JUDGE GEORGE: Thank you Mr. Victor. Mrs. Salisu, the floor is yours.

AMINA SALISU: Thank you Judge George. Humankind has come to a stage where we need to change our mind-set, our way of thinking. Certain laws and norms in our societies must be changed. A girl-child has every right as a boy-child. They should not be given off or forced into early marriages, and in some cases, prostitution.

We have minds that we haven't been able to fully utilise because of the restrictions society has placed on us. If we were given our rights to fully utilise our potentials, the world would be a far greater and better place than it is today. We have done a great many things but because history doesn't remember us, young girls don't have who to aspire to become, young girls don't know their full capabilities.

We need a paradigm shift. Just as a brain is made of two halves working together, women are half the population and we want to work with men to better humanity. And how can we achieve this? Better laws have to be made both for the work environment and the home. We are seeking for better representation in politics. For paternity leaves before and after women give birth. For…

VICTOR ANDREWS: You know that there must be another law to balance paternity leave.

AMINA SALISU: And what is that?

VICTOR ANDREWS: Married couples will not be allowed to work in the same company, be it public or private. No company can afford paid maternity and paternity leaves for women and men.

AMINA SALISU: They would have to. Every person came in…

[One of the workers comes in and signifies Judge George that time is up by touching his watch. Victor and Amina continue arguing.]

JUDGE GEORGE: Well, it seems we will never get to the end of this discussion and that [he pauses] is my judgement. Remember to tune in to KNW 102.5 the best radio station on the planet [the theme song comes on] next Tuesday by 2:30pm. I remain your host, Judge George. See you next week on another exciting program of Judge George.

ACT II
SCENE I

A SHABBY SITTING ROOM. Four chairs and a table. Two children sleeping together on a chair and a third sitting on the ground with his hands on his stomach.
A clock with the time 8:21 hangs on a wall.

[Enter - Judge George]

CHILD 1: Welcome Daddy.

JUDGE GEORGE: Thank you my son. What is going on here? Where is your mother?

CHILD 1: She left immediately after picking us from school and she hasn't returned.

JUDGE GEORGE: [Looks at his watch then the clock on the wall] It is 8:21pm and she is not yet back?

CHILD 1: Daddy we are hungry.

JUDGE GEORGE: She didn't give you anything to eat before she left?

CHILD 1: No she didn't.

JUDGE GEORGE: [Puts his arms akimbo and looks up] What kind of woman is this? Come with me to the kitchen let me fix something for you and your siblings to eat.

[Exit - Judge George and Child 1]

ACT II
SCENE II

The SITTING ROOM is dark. A tipsy woman enters with a bottle in her hand. She stumbles. Judge George switches on the lights. He is seated on a chair.
It is now 01:23am on the clock.

JUDGE GEORGE: Where are you coming from?

THE WIFE: [Startled] Oh George. It is you. I didn't see you.

JUDGE GEORGE: You didn't answer my question. I said, where are you coming from?

THE WIFE: Shhh, you will wake up the kids.

JUDGE GEORGE: The kids? The kids? [He stands up] You left the kids alone for hours to God knows where.

You didn't feed them and now you are worried that they might wake up?

THE WIFE: Shhh [she laughs then hiccups].

JUDGE GEORGE: Where were you?

THE WIFE: I was out, partying with the girls.

JUDGE GEORGE: And because of that you have forgotten your wifely and motherly duties? You think it is normal to come back home at [he looks at the clock] 1:23 in the night?

THE WIFE: I know you will come back and take care of them like you always do.

JUDGE GEORGE: What has become of you? You are not the woman I married.

THE WIFE: [She takes a sip from the bottle] I am exactly the woman you married. You are the one who has changed. Remember how we used to party all day and all night? Remember?

JUDGE GEORGE: But that was a long time ago, we were younger then and we didn't have kids.

THE WIFE: My dear George, you can take the woman out of the club, but you can't take the club out of the woman. Excuse me, I need to… I need to… sleep. [She walks passed Judge George]

JUDGE GEORGE: [He turns towards her in anger] Where are you going? I am still talking to you.

(The wife turns around and throws her bottle at Judge George. He dodges and it hits a wall. He raises his hand and walks towards her but then controls himself and brings it down)

THE WIFE: Hit me, hit me. If you are man enough I said hit me. Exactly, spineless as always.

[Exit - The Wife]

[Judge George walks round the room. He comes to the front of the stage and looks into the audience]

JUDGE GEORGE: AM I A FOOL?

PART 7

The travesty traversed by Travis

	H		■	T		A	
E			Y	■		R	A
	E				D	■	
Y	■		R	A			S

"How much do you love me?" she asked me.

And I replied, "I love you so much that I can't imagine a world where you are my ex."

But today, I live in a world where she is someone's wife. I had been away working in a refugee camp when I got an email from my friend Agbo. I couldn't believe it but he sounded certain. 'Olivia is getting married next week.' The internet had been down for days and phones don't actually work here. The last time Olivia and I spoke we got into an argument. I can't remember why because it had been long and it doesn't really matter, all I wanted after days of cooling off was for us to reconcile and continue from where we left off. But whenever I tried calling her, her number was switched off. I asked Agbo to locate her for me but he couldn't. Had something happened to my baby? I wondered and prayed that nothing bad had befallen her.

Countless number of times I tried calling her but I still got the same answer. Then I was sent to another remote area with no cell coverage and bad internet. And there I stayed for months without a word from anyone until now.

This must be a joke, I said to myself countless number of times. Olivia and I have been making plans on the life we would live. I showed her a picture of the house I would build and the field where our children will play. And she said that was her prayer too. She told me the name she would call our first son, Nelson. Our second she would name Steven with a V not a PH. She didn't like the name I came up with for our daughter so I agreed to disagree sometime in the future when our baby girl arrives.

She told me that all she wanted was me, and that money wouldn't make her happy. She called her home my home. Her mother became a mother to me. I wasn't too close to her siblings but I was close to her mother and we would spend hours talking. It is funny, but I know the story of Olivia right from the womb. The sleepless nights she caused her mother, the kind of food she made her mother crave and the things that happened on the day she was born.

I knew all this, which makes me wonder how on earth she could be getting married to someone that wasn't me. Luckily, I got the email towards the end of my eight months work and a new team was coming to relieve us. I packed my bags, got on the plane and travelled back home, all the while wondering if what Agbo said was true.

I arrived back home safely. It was Easter period and everywhere looked festive. The first person I called after I landed was Olivia's mother. She is usually the mediator whenever Olivia and I have an argument.

"I will talk to her," she usually tells me. But on this day, after I asked her if her daughter was getting married to someone else she had no words to say to me.

"I love your daughter very much and you know that. I will very much like to marry her. I need her new number so that I can talk to her and get her to change her mind."

"Okay, let me see if I have her number," she said, then ended the call.

I got a taxi to take me home. Thirty minutes into the ride she called back.

"Sorry Travis but I don't have her new number," she said, then ended the call.

I couldn't sleep that entire night. The next day was Easter Monday which was also the day for the wedding. I called Agbo and he sent me their wedding invitation. One glance at it my world sunk. If before I doubted it, now I had undisputable evidence. My world had been a lie this passed five years. I wanted to cry, but men don't cry. So I held back my tears; she wasn't worth it.

I put my phone down then it began to ring. It was Olivia's mother.

"Hello," I said, but I got nothing in reply. "Hello? Is somebody there?"

There was no response. This must be a pocket dial so I ended the call and sat in the darkness and brooded. I didn't know when day came, time was a concept I had no understanding of again. There was a knock at the door but it had blended with the noise in the background. I did not notice Agbo when he came in.

"You shouldn't be like this," he said to me, which brought me back to earth.

"Agbo, how can she do this to me?"

"Cheer up Travis. God saved you from something bad," he said to me like it had been said to countless people with broken hearts. "You will get over this."

But how? That is the question. A thought came to me; maybe I could stop this. I could go to the church and when she sees me she will change her mind. But then again, what if she doesn't? That will destroy the last modicum of respect I had for myself. So I held on to my pride, but then my phone rang. It was Olivia's mother calling again.

Agbo and I were shocked when we saw it. I picked it up hoping that it was not another pocket dial. But it was.

"Hello?" I repeated many times, then I cut the call because the message had already been sent. "This is a sign Agbo. I am going to the church. She won't get married if she sees me."

"Travis don't do this," he said, almost kneeling on the ground. "Don't do this to yourself. Nothing good will come of this."

I heard what he said quite alright, but my mind was made up. I took my bath and got dressed in a suit that was suitable for a suitor-turned-husband.

"I am going," I said to Agbo and he didn't mind stopping me.

He hands me my car keys and the spares to my apartment. I got into the car and drove off. Maybe I like suffering, maybe I am addicted to pain. But love isn't love unless it hurts, and true love hurts the most.

My car stopped after ten minutes on the road. It had run out of fuel. Agbo had forgotten to tell me or he did that on purpose. The closest filling station was two miles away. So I ran, with Banky W's *Don't break my heart* playing in my heart. The filling station was open twenty four hours of the day, but on this day, they pasted a sign that says they are closed for Easter. Maybe the owner had become a staunch Christian while I was away.

After fifteen minutes waiting on the road, I finally saw an empty taxi. Have people become more religious while I was away? I wondered. We got to a holdup a mile away from the church. Seriously, did more people find religion while I was away? I had no choice but to come out of the taxi and run the rest of the way. My mind was determined and I felt no fatigue or strain. Maybe I like suffering, maybe I am addicted to pain. But love isn't love unless it hurts, and true love hurts the most. I know, because I came just as Olivia and her husband were coming out of the church. I stood afar from their guests as they cheered.

She who I thought would be my Mrs is now another man's Mrs. She was all smiles while I was all in pain. She ran her eyes through her guests thanking them and then she spotted me. She looked at me like I was a stranger then looked away. It was not like that Michael Learns to Rock song, *25 minutes*. Even if I had arrived twenty five minutes earlier I couldn't have stopped her. Maybe this is why she encouraged and insisted that I take that job that would keep me away for eight months.

I watched the Just Married get into their car and drive off. I stood there for about a minute not knowing what to do. Then I decided that I better leave because there are people who would recognise me. Somehow I found my way home asking myself how could she be so *Heartless?* A question neither I nor Mr. West knew the answer to. Somehow I got to bed like I was in Whitney's *Heartbreak hotel*. Somehow I fell asleep with The Script's *Breakeven* playing in my head.

The next day I woke up and it felt like I was living a dream. It is difficult to *Try sleeping with a broken heart*. This is not the life I envisioned. What does one do when he realises that he had been travelling to a vacuum all the while? Move on? Now I understand Rick Hassani's *Thunder fire you*. I have never been a recluse but I became one for the next week and a half.

"O boy you need to get over what happened," Agbo advised me. "There are many fishes in the sea."

"But dude, she was the one. She was my person," I said, because I have been trying to convince myself like Daniel Bedingfield in *If you're not the one*.

"Maybe she was. But you know what comes after the one?"

"What?"

"The next one."

Maybe he was right, and like James Blunt, I had to say *Goodbye my lover*. But no matter how hard I tried I could not forget her or the lie she made me believe and fall in love with. I am being stalked by pain. Everywhere I go, everything I see, everything I touch, reminds me of her. That song by Savage Garden, *The lover after me*, has become the soundtrack to my life. Brymo is indeed right, *Heartbreak songs are better in English*. I need something uplifting. Eminem's *Puke, Same song and dance* comes to mind.

I went back into the world. My friends and family knew what happened so they never broached the subject. There was a light, spark or enthusiasm in me that was dead. I still found women beautiful and attractive, but it was only physical and I wanted more than that. I even gave up on meeting my celebrity crush. I had no interest in flirting especially when Agbo drags me to clubs like we are now.

"How about that girl there?" Agbo asked, as he pointed at a girl.

"No, I am not interested," I said, being the death of the party as usual.

"How about this one?"

"No."

"And this one?"

"You and I have different tastes. You like women that are buxom."

"Yes I do. I must marry a woman with big boobs, otherwise I will not have peace of mind. If you are not going to talk to any of them then I better do."

Agbo went on his merry way while I got out my phone. I am the only one in the club sitting down and going through his phone. Olivia has been *happily married and living the blessed life* for three months now as she says on her bio. There are hundreds of pictures from their honeymoon with her husband tagged. The most recent was posted five minutes ago from a Chinese restaurant with the caption - *God, their is no one loke you.* Yes, in those exact words.

"Why are you still stalking your ex on social media?" asked Agbo, which startled me.

"I am not stalking her."

"Then what are you doing?"

"I am looking at her wedding pictures, and I will continue to do so until they hurt no more."

And the truth is, it hurts less now.

"I think I should be going home now. There is no point of me being here."

Surprisingly, Agbo didn't disagree.

"Let me know when you get home okay?" he said.

"Sure. Here, take my car." I tossed my car keys. "By the time you leave here commercial vehicles would no longer be on the road."

I boarded a bus so that I could think and I didn't want to do that while driving. We were only two passengers in the bus.

"Stop thinking," the other passenger said. She was a lady.

"Excuse me?"

"You need to get over it," she said to me, authoritatively.

"What makes you think that I have something on my mind?"

"I am psychic," she said, with a grin on her face.

"I think you should mind your business."

"How can someone ewho is telepathic mind their business when your thoughts are screaming at her?"

I couldn't tell if she was joking or serious. But I decided to humour myself.

"So what am I thinking now?" I asked.

"You are wondering if I am serious or joking."

My mouth opened as my eyes widened. I composed myself so that she wouldn't know that she was right. Or maybe she did, or maybe she didn't. I don't know. She has got me discombobulated and I didn't want to ask another question for fear that she may indeed be a psychic.

"What are you reading?" I asked.

"Nothing that you will be interested in."

"Try me."

"It is about the effect of neo-colonialism and linguistic erosion/usurpation in sub-Saharan Africa with emphasis on the Horn of Africa."

"Wow, that's interesting," I said, and she saw through my façade and smiled.

We talked for what seemed like hours though it was minutes. I didn't understand some of what she said, but I liked the joy and passion in her voice. Her stop was coming up she told me and I didn't want our conversation to end. Do I ask for her number or not? When I follow my heart I fail. When I do what my head says, I fail. So tell me, what am I to do?

"Can I have your number?" I asked, I don't know if it is my heart or my head talking.

Martin Eloke Chukwumah

She tore a page from her book and began to draw lines.

"What are you doing?" I asked, but she said nothing.

Two minutes later she gives me the piece of paper with a bunch of numbers on it.

	8	3		1	9	5	7	
7	II			4				8
	6		IX		7	1	9	
	2	VII		3	1	4		
1	3	4		2	IV	8	6	7
	5		4	7	8	3		VI
6	9						VIII	
V		5		I		3		8	1
3		8	1	9		III	2	5

"What is this?"

"A game of Sudoku. Complete it and you will get my phone number."

"I don't understand."

"You see those Roman numerals?"

"Yes."

"Whatever number you find in that box, the Roman numeral there will tell you the order in which it appears on my phone number. For example, the box marked V, whatever number you find there is the fifth number of my phone number. And so on and so forth."

"Are you serious?"

"Yes. We have arrived at my stop."

"Wouldn't it be easier for you to just write your phone number down?"

"Oh Travis, you need to see the world from a different perspective. It is the only way you can come out of the gloomy place you are in. You need more light in your life, and I will help you find it." She paused for two seconds then said, "You are lucky that I gave you a 9x9 puzzle instead of a 16x16 puzzle. Goodnight."

"Wait, what is your name?" I asked, but she had already alighted.

I watched through the window as this lady walked away. I told her my name but she never told me hers. I looked at the bus driver and saw him smiling from the rear-view mirror. I got home and the first thing I did was get out my pen and began to solve the puzzle given to me by the mysterious and puzzling woman. I hope that whatever number I get is her real one. It will be annoying if at the end she had given me a fake number.

It had been ages since I played Sudoku but I managed to complete it. It was around midnight but I had to quench my curiosity and find out if the number was real or fake. So I called, and surprisingly it was ringing. I thought about hanging up but then she picked.

"Hello Travis," she said.

"How did you know it was me?"

"You ask this question still?"

We talked through the night until the sun pierced the clouds with its fingers. We made a date in two days time.

"So what is your name? I need to know who I have been speaking to all through the night."

"I will tell you on our date. Goodnight, or good morning… goodbye."

She cut the call. I sat in silence for minutes wondering about this woman. What name do I use to save her number? Why is she so mysterious? These questions and more followed me to my dream as I dreamt of our date.

I woke up around noon, brushed, took my bath and ate. I had to tell someone about this lady. Agbo should be home by now, so I went to see him. His house isn't far from mine. I walked in as he was working out. He was on this new regimen and it was showing.

"You wouldn't believe what happened to me after I left the club."

"What happened?"

"I will tell you after you are done. It is quite interesting."

After he had his bath his mind was clear so I told him.

"I told you you will fall in love again," he said.

"I never said I was in love."

"You didn't have to. It is written all over your face. You may deny it all you want but your body proves the contrary."

"I don't care what you have to say. Are we going to see your grandmother or not?"

"Yes, but I have to put some things in order first."

Two hours later we were at the hospital. His grandmother was recovering from hip replacement surgery. She and her late husband raised Agbo. His father died when he was five and his mother was barely in the picture even till this day.

"Good afternoon ma," I greeted, as Agbo did the same but added a hug. "How are you feeling today?"

"Better than yesterday," she answered. "What happened? I didn't see you yesterday."

"Sorry ma."

"That's okay, I forgive you," she said, then we both laughed.

"You wouldn't be seeing much of him grandma. Travis has fallen in love with the mysterious lady he met last night."

"No I haven't."

"Yes you have. You told me that it was love at first sight."

"No I didn't."

"Yes, you did."

"No I didn't."

"Boys will never change," said the grandmother. "Travis."

"Yes?"

"Love at first sight is easy. Love at last sight, that is hard. If after you have experienced life with someone and you still love them, then, that is love. That is what I had with his grandfather. He died right here in my arms, and as he took his last breath, he looked at me. I was not a good wife but in his eyes I saw love. Don't get me wrong, there is nothing wrong with love at first sight. But ask yourself, do you see love at last sight with this lady?"

That question remained with me till my date with the lady of mystery. We met at her bus stop. She was dressed almost the same way as she was the last time I saw her but she looked more beautiful.

"You look beautiful," I had to put words to my thoughts.

"Thank you," she said, like she doubted my words. "So tell me, what name did you save my number with?"

"Mystique," I answered.

"Oh really?" she said, laughing. "That was my nickname is secondary school."

"So what is your name?"

"I will tell you at the end of our date, I promise."

She picked the place for our first date. It was a poetry event. She introduced me to her friends only after she instructed them not to tell me her name. They all seemed chummy and for some reason I sensed that this is the first she has brought a man to the show.

They were all poets and performed their poems in their native tongues. Mystique was a poet also, and when it came to her turn, she performed in four different languages, Igbo, Hausa, Yoruba. I didn't know what the fourth was.

"It is Swahili and Idoma," her friend Titi said. "You looked confused."

"So she spoke five languages not four."

"Yes."

"I only understood the Yoruba and Igbo. I was lost for the rest of it. How many languages can she speak?"

"I absolutely have no idea."

"What's the message of her poem?"

"She never tells us everything. You have to research to find out. You see people recording her right?"

"Yes."

"They go back and study her words to get her messages which are quite moving and deep when you decipher what she said."

It was an interesting first date and as we walked back, she told me the meaning of her poem.

"It is about the construct of life," she said. "Take away religion. Take away politics. Take away money. Take away fashion. And you will still have life left, maybe in its purest form. We created all these as the definition of life. Take away love. Take away hope. Take away perseverance. What do you have left? Nothing."

"So you are an atheist?"

"No, don't get me wrong. I believe in God. If God doesn't exist then where does our capacity to love come from? God is not a religion, God is Love, Hope and Perseverance."

"That is the title of your poem."

"Yes, but written and spoken in three different languages."

She hands me a paper when we came to the junction where we would part ways.

"What is this?" I asked.

"My name," she said, as she walked away.

I opened the paper and it was the same thing.

I	D		[4]	E	B	H		
A				F	G	B	C	I
	F		A		[1]	[3]	D	G
D			H	B	E			F
	G	[6]		A	D	C	E	[5]
E	H			I			B	D
[2]						D	H	
		D	B		F	G		
G	C	A	E		H		I	B

— — — — — —

"Your name has a nice meaning," I called her later that night after I had solved the puzzle.

"Thank you."

"But I like Mystique better," I said, and she laughed.

We went on more dates and she began to let me in. She was simple and mysterious, homely and otherworldly at the same time. She met my friends and they all liked her more than they liked She-Who-Will-No-Longer-Be Named. My lady of mystery or She-Who-Kept-Her-Name-A-Mystery was yet to visit my apartment. She had a rule; Never visit a guy until you know his mother's maiden name. This goes for guys without hyphens in their surname or whose parents are not divorced.

I was filling a form for my next assignment in her apartment when she saw my mother's maiden name and that was when she told me her rule and we fixed a date for her visit. I was supposed to pick her but she had a previous engagement so I sent her my home address.

"What is this?" She asked.
"My home address."
"You live in a website?"
"No, just scan the code and you will see my address. I will be waiting for you. Bye."

She arrived and the first thing she said was, "You are funny."

She had given me a list of ingredients to buy and I had them ready in the kitchen. After a quick tour which ended in the kitchen she asked for my apron and began cooking. She asked me to stay and keep her company but not to touch anything. I had an uncanny talent for burning my food. My stomach was filled with the sweet aroma before the meal was ready. She dished the meal and mine was twice the quantity of hers.

"Here," she said, as she emptied half of her plate in mine. "I am not that hungry."

I laughed and thanked her. The meal was indeed delicious but I don't know if I enjoyed the food or our conversation more. It is true what my people say; the way to a man's heart is through his stomach. I had been stomaching a feeling for a while and now that my stomach was filled, I let it out.

"I love you," I said.

She was completely silent. I don't know if she was in shock or happy to hear my truth. I just wish she could say something because it is becoming awkward. The vibration of her phone broke the silence.

"Titi is calling me," she said, then picked the call. "Hello?"

I was sitting next to her but I paid no attention to what she was saying until she tapped me on the shoulder.

"Titi just told that one of my spoken word performances has gotten over a hundred thousand views."

"Really?"

"Yes, she sent me the link."

She clicked on it and we saw the video. There were thousands of comments and thumbs-up with a few haters giving it thumbs-down.

"When did you post it?"

"I didn't. I guess it is one of our guests who posted it online and it is getting noticed."

A hundred thousand views was just the beginning as it went north of fifty million. She has gone viral.

"I don't like that word," she said to me.

"What word?"

"Viral. Viral is when a virus spreads. My message is not a virus. It is my innermost thoughts that I want to share with people and bring enlightenment to the world."

She had seventeen poetry books published which had gone unnoticed. But now, orders were coming in the thousands, calls were coming from agents who would like to represent her and invites were coming from all over the world because her poems were written in many languages and they wanted her to talk about her philosophy, the themes, messages of her poems and so on.

I was indeed happy for her. We have been together a little over a year now and just as we got this good news we were hit by a not so good one. I have been called back for another eight months. I had a month before I travel so we used this time the best we could. She and Agbo accompanied me to the airport. They stayed with me until twenty minutes before my flight.

"Take care of yourself," Agbo said.

"I will miss you," she said.

"I will miss you both."

"But I won't miss you," joked Agbo.

We shook and hugged goodbye, then I hugged her and said, "I love you."

She said nothing in return. I climbed on the escalator and when I was half way up I looked back and then I realised that I could see my love at last sight with her. As we were boarding I got a message from her.

I didn't need to scan it to know what it was.

We communicated everyday and she sent me a poem every night. This is one of them.

We have been apart for four months now and I pray for the next four months to go fast because I want to join her in whatever country she's in. Her call came in one afternoon during my break but the network was bad.

"Tell me, how was Chile?" I asked.

"What?"

"I said, how was Chile?"
"It was fine. I am travelling though."
"To where?" I asked, then the line was cut.
She sent me this picture.

I scanned it and did as asked, then I saw her live and in person. I left my lunch and went and hugged her.

"How did you get here? I thought you were going to Colombia next."

"That can wait, I wanted to see you and not just through the phone. Luckily I met someone in your organisation and she was able to send me here as a volunteer."

She came just at the right time because six thousand one hundred and sixty five refugees just came into the camp. Two hundred and twenty seven volunteers were recruited with forty three of them being medical officers. She was of great help, especially with the children. Whenever I look at her,

One Direction's *What makes you beautiful* and Uncle Sam's *When I see you smile* come to mind. She was not only the light of my life, but the light to everyone she meets.

On her sixth week in the camp, after we finished a meeting, I handed her a report on the children which she had requested for.

"Oh good," she said, as she began to go through it. "I think I have an idea on how to structure their…"

She stopped speaking because she saw this image printed on a paper.

She scanned it then looked at me.

"You were right when you said you will bring light into my life," I said. "Because before you I thought that I was happy, I thought I was loved, but it was all a lie, a travesty of love. You show me what life and love is. I am not as poetic as you but I speak the truth from my heart. And I want us to spend the rest of our lives together and in the afterlife also because I don't think God will ever separate us."

She laughs.

"So what do you say? What is your answer?"

"Yes," she answered. "A thousand times yes."

She embraced me with tears of joy in her eyes.

"I don't want a big wedding," she said.

"Are you sure? We both come from large families."

"It may be big, it may be small, I really don't care. But what I want is for it to be meaningful."

"And meaningful it will be."

We both called home and shared the news with our families. She still had some touring to do, and after that we would get married. Agbo too has found a lady he would like to marry and I was eager to meet her.

My fiancée spent another week in the camp before she resumed her tour. We were apart but I can honestly tell you that I smelled her perfume everywhere I went and knew what she was eating when she was eating it. I would call and she would ask me how I knew. And the truth is, some things can't be explained.

My eight months in the camp came to an end and I went back home, this time with a smile and not panicking. Agbo picked me up at the airport. On our way he picked up his girlfriend.

"This is Jane," he introduced her to me.

There was something I noticed about her but I had to wait until he dropped her off at her workplace before I asked.

"I thought you said you must marry a woman with big boobs?"

"I did but, Jane gives me peace of mind, and I wouldn't trade that for anything or maltreat her in any way."

We talked about my wedding the rest of the way.

The months went by quickly and my wedding was just a couple of hours away. Last night my wife-to-be sent me this poem.

I didn't get some of it. I will ask her to explain when she becomes my Mrs. It was a beehive of activities that day that not even I the groom found space in my own house. I booked a hotel room where I and Agbo my best man stayed. He was away performing his best man duties when I heard a knock at the door. Why was he knocking? I asked myself. Then I went and opened it and to my surprise it was She-Who-Will-No-Longer-Be-Named. I have not seen her in years and have forgotten that she existed, honestly.

"May I come in?" she asked, but came in even though I said nothing.

It is like *The man who can't be moved* by The Script has finally gotten his wish.

"What are you doing here?" I asked.

"Travis don't marry her."

"Excuse me?"

"I am sorry for what I did to you. I am willing to leave my husband this very moment if you call off your wedding."

"You must be joking."

"No I am not. I am dead serious. My husband is a monster, my marriage is hell. It is the biggest mistake of my life."

"But you looked so happy and fulfilled."

"That's all a façade. I pretend so that the world wouldn't know what I am going through. But now I want out. I want you back. You are the only one who ever treated me nice, with love and respect. I thought I knew what I wanted then but now I am older and wiser and I realise my mistake. Travis don't get married to her. You are my soulmate, we belong together. You remember the plans we made, don't you?"

"That was a long time ago, in the past."

"It could still be our future. It is what I think of when I am sad. It is what gives me hope. Travis please come back to me, come back to me and let's continue from where we left off."

She kneels down and begins to beg.

"Please get up, get up," I said, then lifted her to her feet.

"We belong together Travis and you know it. Don't make the same mistake I did. We can course-correct."

It took all the strength in me not to laugh at this very moment.

"I love my wife. There is nothing that you can do or say that will make me change my mind. I thought I would never recover after what you did to me but then I must thank you. Because if not for that, I wouldn't have met my wife. So thank you."

My last words caught her by surprise. She remained speechless until she left the room a few seconds later. I exhaled after she left. I couldn't believe what just happened. I continued my preparations. The love of my life is waiting for me, and I couldn't wait to make her mine.

She wore her mother's wedding dress, the beads of her grandmothers, the high heels of her favourite aunt, the wrist watch of her late father and my love in her heart. She faced me and we stood before God and our families and took our vows. I said mine in English while she said hers in Igbo and Yoruba. This is the happiest I have ever been in my life.

We had our reception in her family compound. It was spacious and well decorated that guests asked if they too could hold an event here. Time came for our first dance as a married couple. We walked together to the dance floor and the Disc Jockey played nice songs unlike the ones that had defined my life some years back. People came and sprayed us with money. They all went back to their seats when the slow songs came on. I held my wife and we danced, matching each other's step and rhythm.

As we turned, I saw She-Who-Will-No-Longer-Be-Named looking at us as I looked at her on her wedding day. I know that there is only one thing in her mind. I know she wonders,

www.ingramcontent.com/pod-product-compliance
Lightning Source LLC
Chambersburg PA
CBHW021944120726
47992CB00001B/129